MW01690520

An Audience with the King

Putting the Fire Back in Your Prayer Life

Rick Bezanson

An Audience with the King

Putting the Fire Back Into Your Prayer Life

© 2012 Rick Bezanson

ISBN: 978-0-9856234-0-1

Unless otherwise indicated, Bible quotations are taken from the *New International Version of the Bible*. Copyright 1973, 1978, 1984 by Zondervan Publishing.

Format/Cover Design: Minion Editing & Design
www.joyminion.com

Contents

Dedication

This book is dedicated to our Lord Jesus Christ, who took a very prodigal son and transformed him into a Reverend Doctor.
All glory be to God and the Lamb forever.

I also dedicate this book to my beautiful wife Robyn, my greatest blessing,

and to my two wonderful sons Ricky and Ryan, my pride and joy.

Preface

Twenty-five years ago, if someone would have told me I would be writing my second Christian book, I would have asked, "What have you been smoking?" For 25 years ago, I was, as Hank Williams Jr. would say, "whiskey bent and hell bound." I was a functional alcoholic with a beautiful wife, two great kids, a great job, a new home and two new cars in the driveway.

Then an amazing thing happened. One night after returning home from a family party (after consuming a twelve pack of beer), I lay next to my sleeping wife and began to cry. I was tired of the emptiness brought on from the booze. I was tired of my numbing existence. As I wept, I prayed, "Jesus, if you are there, then take my life because I don't want it." Little did I know how that simple prayer of little faith would change my life. The next day I quit drinking, and at the urging of my pastor I started to read the Bible. Through the Scriptures I came to know Jesus—and my life was changed forever. I started to live the ever-changing adventure of Jesus.

My priorities in life were changed—now the most important thing in life for me was to introduce people to Jesus. I knew He was real. Although our eternal destination was important, I wanted people to know Jesus here and now so they could experience real life in the present.

This experience led me to Fuller Theological Seminary and Pacific Lutheran Theological Seminary, and eventually to ordination in the Evangelical Lutheran Church in America (ELCA). The adventure of living with Jesus led me into urban ministry, Latino ministry and the Lutheran Congregations in Mission for Christ (LCMC). Jesus taught me a new language: Spanish. (I had never liked languages, although I'd studied four years of French in high school.)

All I ever wanted was a call to a nice little church in the suburbs—with maybe 150-200 members who all spoke English, a sanctuary and classrooms that were paid for, one or two services on Sunday, and an opportunity to reach people for Jesus in a domesticated arena. However, The Lord Jesus had other plans for me.

I have served as a pastor for 15 years—in the city, in a multicultural setting, in churches where monies for mission are scarce and multiple and varied worship services are necessary—reaching people for Jesus whom other churches might not want.

God led me to serve the poor, those with little or no education, those with addictions and untreated family problems, the illegal aliens, the divorced, the incarcerated, single parent families, unmarried cohabitating couples with children and the mentally challenged.

Later the Lord led me into the toughest jail complex in America, the Maricopa County jails, where we currently have five jail churches.

During this journey my prayer life went from periods of experiencing the presence and power of God in a very intimate relationship to periods of spiritual dryness where God felt distant and removed. At these times it felt like I was praying in a spiritual vacuum.

The purpose of this book is to share my adventure in prayer and to encourage readers to go deeper in prayer and in their loving relationship with the Father, Son, and Holy Spirit.

My prayer is that this book will provide readers with an understanding of what prayer really is, and also nurture a spiritual hunger for it. Prayer is not a duty or obligation—it is a time of presence and power. May the Spirit guide and empower you as you read this work.

Chapter One

Introduction: The Eye Opening Journey

I am not a mystic or a spiritual guru in the body of Christ, the church. I am an urban pastor, who by God's grace has been called to serve Jesus in a multicultural, diverse and financially depressed environment. I preach six times a week (twice in Spanish), lead three Bible studies per week, lead a prayer meeting, mentor our Bubba Scouts (boy's group), lead two jail churches, go on visitations, counsel people in jail and in the church, and perform administrative duties as the full-time pastor. Also, we are planning to start a second church site in a care center. I am not complaining or bragging, but simply stating what our Lord empowers me to do.

I was not always on fire for prayer. Being raised in the Roman Catholic Church, most of my prayers as a child and youth were rote prayers—primarily the Lord's Prayer, Hail Mary, and Glory Be. I don't wish to debate the effectiveness of these prayers, but I do know that God heard me. Later in life, when I was in my 30s, our Lord Jesus heard my prayer and healed me of an addiction to alcohol. I was attending a Missouri Synod Lutheran

Church at the time, and was discipled by Pastor Chuck Meyer. It is at this time that I began reading God's Word and discovered Jesus is real. Like all newborn Christians, I was flooded with the peace of Christ and the fire of the Holy Spirit. I wanted all people to have a relationship with Jesus. At the same time, I was hungry for more of Jesus. I found myself talking to Jesus all the time!

Then Jackie, an elderly saint at our church, recommended we have a prayer vigil. I didn't know what a prayer vigil was, but I knew it was about Jesus so I volunteered to lead it. We started with a sign up sheet, with the goal of having someone praying in the sanctuary every hour of a 24-hour period. We were a small church, so I wasn't surprised when the midnight to five a.m. slots on the chart were blank. I was not discouraged. I signed up for the remaining hours.

In the quiet of the sanctuary I prostrated myself before the Lord. I prayed out loud, read the psalms, sang hymns—it was good no one else was in the building because no one should be subjected to my singing—and listened to God. The hours I spent in the sanctuary seemed like minutes. I was filled to overflowing with the Holy Spirit. I felt completely at peace and invincible, unshakable and full of energy and power. I remember thinking at the time that if someone punched me in the face, I would simply say, "God bless you!" In the many prayer vigils that followed, my wife Robyn and I both experienced the power and peace of God's presence in the dimly-lit sanctuary.

Not long after this experience and at the prompting of Pastor Chuck and our Lord, I started my studies at Fuller Theological seminary to become a pastor. My family thought I was nuts. Robyn prayed that I would get this whole "pastor thing" out of my head.

While at Fuller I started keeping a prayer journal that I still use every day. I set aside an hour a day for prayer—a discipline I still keep. I went to Pacific Lutheran Theological Seminary (PLTS) in Berkeley, California, to fulfill my one year at a Lutheran seminary.

My faithful wife Robyn stayed in Phoenix with our two boys during this time—it was the most difficult year in our family's life together. I think Robyn is a saint. I fought depression by praying more and turning to the Psalms. To this day I still favor the Psalms of lament in the Psalter.

I continued the discipline of prayer every morning throughout my first call, and into my second call at Amazing Grace Christian Church in Phoenix. But there were many times when my prayer time seemed dry and lifeless. Where had all the bells and whistles gone?

While at Fuller I read *Fresh Wind, Fresh Fire* by Jim Cymbala. That book completely changed my view and practice of prayer. At the same time I read *Listening to God* and *The Voice of Jesus* by Gordon T. Smith.

During this period the Lord blessed me with Dr. Perry Kopatz as a part-time co-pastor. Perry received his doctorate from the Wagner Institute and has helped our church—and me—to understand better the gifts of the Holy Spirit.

We started a Monday evening prayer meeting at Amazing Grace. (I'll refer to this prayer time often in the following pages.) Although the service agenda fluctuates, generally it consists of a private time of prayer and confession, followed by Holy Communion. Then we have a time of prayer walks and corporate prayer. People pray sitting, kneeling, walking or prostrate on the floor. Some pray aloud, some quietly, and some in tongues.

The atmosphere is similar to the Tuesday night prayer meetings described by Pastor Jim Cymbala at his congregation, the Brooklyn Tabernacle:

As the meeting edges to a close, I overhear mothers petitioning for wayward children ... men asking God to please help them find employment ... others giving thanks for recent answers to prayer ... tearful voices here and there. I can't help but think, *This is as close to heaven as I will ever get in this life. I don't want to leave here. If I were invited to the White House to meet some dignitary, it would never bring the kind of peace and deep joy I sense here in the presence of people calling on the Lord.*[1]

The prayer service at Amazing Grace lasts between one and two-and-a-half hours. This extremely powerful ministry of the mother church has led to the expansion of existing ministries. Up to 20 people pray on Mondays. (I must emphasize here that numbers are not important.) These brothers and sisters who pray on Monday evenings are the prayer "special forces" of Amazing Grace. Occasionally, these prayer warriors will do prayer walks around the church grounds or neighborhood. Their presence, encouragement, and prayers remind me of Moses with Hur and Aaron in Exodus during the battle with the Amalekites. Pastors—even if you are the only one who shows up, you need to be willing to pray. You will be blessed. You will receive the power of the Holy Spirit.

Exodus 17:10-13 states:

> *So Joshua fought the Amalekites as Moses had ordered, and Moses, Aaron and Hur went to the top of the hill.*
>
> *As long as Moses held up his hands, the Israelites were winning, but whenever he lowered his hands, the Amalekites were winning.*
>
> ***When Moses' hands grew tired, they took a stone and put it under him and he sat on***

it. Aaron and Hur held his hands up—one on one side, one on the other—so that his hands remained steady till sunset.

So Joshua overcame the Amalekite army with the sword. (Emphasis added)

In a similar manner, our prayer warriors keep the pastors' arms raised in prayer as we engage the spiritual forces of darkness. Since initiating this prayer time on Monday nights, the Spirit has been unleashed at Amazing Grace, changing and spiritually growing both the membership and the ministries. It has changed our church, Dr. Kopatz, and me substantially.

This past year Pastor Kopatz and I did a sermon series on prayer to encourage our members in their prayer lives. The response of those who heard the message was so positive that I felt the Spirit calling me to write this book, based on the series of sermons. In the following pages I will define prayer, the power of prayer, how to pray, obedience and prayer, and the awareness of God and His timing.

I write this not as an expert or completely sanctified saint, but as a simple man who has been granted an audience with the King. If you are looking for numerical growth in members and dollars, this book is not for you. If you want to grow in your faith, in the power of the Holy Spirit—and grow other disciples—then dig in.

My hope is that this book will put the Fire of the Holy Spirit into you and your church. I pray this book will be a means for you to experience an even deeper and more powerful relationship with the King. My purpose is that you would "*Taste and see that the LORD is good; blessed is the man who takes refuge in him.*" — Psalm 34:8

Discussion or Reflection Questions:

1. Have you ever experienced the overwhelming power, peace and presence of God in prayer? Please describe.

2. Have you ever felt abandoned by God? Describe a time when God has seemed distant and your prayers were dry.

3. Read Psalm13 and discuss.

4. How has your own prayer life evolved?

5. Have you ever experienced spiritual warfare? Who has been your Aaron and/or Hur? Please describe.

Chapter Two

The Definition of Prayer

When I first developed this preaching series with my brother in Christ, Pastor Perry Kopatz, I hoped he would be the one to start the series with a definition of prayer. After all, I am evangelical, charismatic, and Lutheran, while Perry is charismatic, evangelical, and Lutheran. We all know those charismatic mystical types are much better at prayer, right?

Well, God had a different idea, so I began to investigate the subject of prayer. According to the *American Heritage Dictionary*, prayer is "a reverent petition made to a deity." When I read this definition, I understood why most people struggle with prayer. This definition made prayer sound as exciting as watching paint dry.

I realized that most people don't pray because they have never really understood prayer, let alone experienced it—like Christians who have been members of the Christian faith their entire lives, but never experienced or lived in a personal relationship with Jesus Christ.

I reviewed my notes on Jim Cymbala and Gordon T. Smith. Cymbala's concept of entering the throne room of grace in prayer captivated me. I started searching the Scriptures. I focused on the psalms, the prayers of God's people for 3,000 years. Psalm 34 really sums up prayer. It is interesting that David wrote this after pretending to be insane. Perhaps we need to include a little divine insanity into our prayers. Maybe our prayers would be more powerful and effective if we stepped outside of the box, outside of our comfort zones. Maybe we could try standing, kneeling, laying down, raising our hands, using a different language, etc.

Psalm 34

Of David. When he pretended to be insane before Abimelech, who drove him away, and he left.

I will extol the Lord at all times; his praise will always be on my lips.

My soul will boast in the Lord; let the afflicted hear and rejoice.

Glorify the Lord with me; let us exalt his name together.

I sought the Lord, and he answered me; he delivered me from all my fears.

Those who look to him are radiant; their faces are never covered with shame.

This poor man called, and the Lord heard him; he saved him out of all his troubles.

The angel of the Lord encamps around those who fear him, and he delivers them.

Taste and see that the Lord is good; blessed is the man who takes refuge in him.

Fear the Lord, you his saints, for those who fear him lack nothing.

The lions may grow weak and hungry, but those who seek the LORD lack no good thing.

Come, my children, listen to me; I will teach you the fear of the LORD.

Whoever of you loves life and desires to see many good days,

keep your tongue from evil and your lips from speaking lies.

Turn from evil and do good; seek peace and pursue it.

The eyes of the LORD are on the righteous and his ears are attentive to their cry;

the face of the LORD is against those who do evil, to cut off the memory of them from the earth.

The righteous cry out, and the LORD hears them; he delivers them from all their troubles.

The LORD is close to the brokenhearted and saves those who are crushed in spirit.

A righteous man may have many troubles, but the LORD delivers him from them all;

he protects all his bones, not one of them will be broken.

Evil will slay the wicked; the foes of the righteous will be condemned.

The LORD redeems his servants; no one will be condemned who takes refuge in him.

From my study of Psalm 34 and many other Scriptures, I arrived at the following definition of prayer:

> Prayer is seeking the Lord, entering His presence through Jesus Christ, and having a heart-to-heart conversation with God guided by the Holy Spirit that leads to transformation.

We will look at every aspect of this definition, and hopefully gain a better understanding of the gift of prayer.

Prayer is Seeking the Lord

> ***I sought the Lord, and he answered me; he delivered me from all my fears.***
> — Psalm 34:4 (Emphasis added.)

The first thing we do is seek the Lord. David writes, "*I sought the Lord, and he answered me; he delivered me from all my fears*" (Psalm 34:4). The image of seeking the face of the Lord or calling upon the Lord is that of a person seeking an audience with a king or ruler. When we see the face of the king—when we get an audience—then our request will be heard. The following Scriptures illustrate this point.

> *My heart says of you, "Seek his face!" Your face, Lord, I will seek.*
>
> *Do not hide your face from me, do not turn your servant away in anger; you have been my helper. Do not reject me or forsake me, O God my Savior.*
> — Psalm 27:8-9

> *Look to the Lord and his strength; seek his face always.* — Psalm 105:4

> *Restore us, O God; make your face shine upon us, that we may be saved.* — Psalm 80:3

> *The Lord make his face shine upon you and be gracious to you; the Lord turn his face toward you and give you peace. — Numbers 6:25-26*

> *During the reign of David, there was a famine for three successive years; so David sought the face*

of the LORD. The LORD said, "It is on account of Saul and his blood-stained house; it is because he put the Gibeonites to death. —2 Samuel 21:1

Look to the LORD and his strength; seek his face always. — 1 Chronicles 16:11

If my people, who are called by my name, will humble themselves and pray and seek my face and turn from their wicked ways, then will I hear from heaven and will forgive their sin and will heal their land. — 2 Chronicles 7:14

It is an ongoing theme in the Bible to seek the face of the Lord. Time and time again the Lord God, through His prophets, implores His people to seek His face. God wants us to seek an audience with Him. He wants us to spend time in prayer with Him. The Everlasting God and Creator of all wants us to desire an audience with Him. How can this possibly be boring? Can we make time for God?

So, how do we seek the face of God? After all, isn't the King of all creation distant or removed from us? Isn't God enthroned in heaven doing His "God stuff"? Yes, God is enthroned in heaven, but He is also present with us. The Scriptures attest to God's closeness to His people.

Where can I go from your Spirit? Where can I flee from your presence? — Psalm 139:7

Be still, and know that I am God; I will be exalted among the nations, I will be exalted in the earth.

The LORD Almighty is with us; the God of Jacob is our fortress. —Psalm 46:10-11

*The LORD replied, "**My Presence will go with you,** and I will give you rest."* — Exodus 33:14 (Emphasis added.)

The children of your servants will live in your presence; their descendants will be established before you." — Psalm 102:28 (Emphasis added.)

The Lord God is always with us. Therefore, when we seek the King's face, we simply cannot miss it because God is present with us. Ignoring the Lord's presence is a major stumbling block in prayer and in the life of a Christian. The Lord is with us! Please seek His face!

Jesus stated in John 11:41-42:

...Father, I thank you that you have heard me, ***I knew that you always hear me***.

I said this for the benefit of the people standing here, that they may believe that you sent me. (Emphasis added.)

The Lord is with us and hears us!

Entering His presence through Jesus Christ

David writes,

Is anyone crying for help? God is listening, ready to rescue you.

If your heart is broken, you'll find God right there; if you're kicked in the gut, he'll help you catch your breath.

— Psalm 34:17-18 (*Message*)

God is continually present with us, so when we seek His face we don't have to go to some faraway place or sanctuary. We simply ask for an audience with the King. God is present with us, and we, as Christians, have special access. We have an intercessor who presents us to the King. All Christians have access to the King through Jesus Christ.

Therefore, since we have a great high priest who has gone through the heavens, Jesus the Son of God, let us hold firmly to the faith we profess.

For we do not have a high priest who is unable to sympathize with our weaknesses, but we have one who has been tempted in every way, just as we are—yet was without sin.

Let us then approach the throne of grace with confidence, so that we may receive mercy and find grace to help us in our time of need.

— Hebrews 4:14-16

To him* [Jesus] *who is able to keep you from stumbling and to present you before his glorious presence without fault and with great joy... — Jude 1:24 (Emphasis added.)

And everyone who calls on the name of the Lord [Jesus] *will be saved.* — Acts 2:21

We have immediate access to God's throne of Grace because of the blood of Jesus. ***The most important aspect of prayer is that it brings us into God's presence.*** Our Monday evening prayer meetings usually begin with 30-40 minutes of silence. During this time of silence we experience the Lord's presence in a very powerful way. His presence is real, and affects people in different ways. Some feel warmth or a tingling sensation throughout their bodies. Others get goose bumps, feel a tingling in their scalps, or feel the hairs on the back of their necks go up. Still others feel warmth and power in their hands. Some people feel weak, and may actually fall over. Many pray with groans or in tongues. Some hear God's voice. Others feel flooded with light, and some see angels.

Most commonly, however, God's presence is usually accompanied with an overwhelming sense of peace, well-being and power. The power feels like a type of energy—almost electrical—that fills our bodies and passes through us to others when we intercede for them. It is an astounding phenomenon. We should not be afraid of feeling emotional or experiencing a host of different feelings. Our emotions and feelings are an integral part of being in God's presence. Our emotions and feelings affirm that God is real and present, and ready to guide us. We must listen with our emotions and feelings if we want God to guide our steps.

While this listening process involves the emotions of the group, it also involves reason.

Gordon T. Smith explains,

> God does not have a mouth; He does not speak audibly. Rather, God speaks to us through our feelings, impressions left on our minds. But we must not equate the voice in our head with the voice of God. We rather discern God's word in the interpretation of these impressions. We discern by perceiving and evaluating the movements of the heart. In the end it will be reason that guides us—but reason comes to terms with the feelings and impressions that are left on our inner person.[2]

At Amazing Grace, we use both our emotions and our reason. Emotions are not something to fear, but a means of listening to God. Emotions are to be embraced. We function with reason, but also listen to our instinctual gut feelings—this is one way in which God communicates with us.

Having a Heart-to-Heart Conversation with God, Guided by the Holy Spirit

When I was desperate, I called out, and God got me out of a tight spot.
— Psalm 34:6 (*Message*) (Emphasis added.)

After our period of silence and realizing God's presence and peace, we usually are flooded with petitions, prayers, praises or laments. I believe this flood of ideas is direct guidance from the Holy Spirit. We enter into a heart-to-heart talk with God, and the Holy Spirit guides this conversation.

For those who are led by the Spirit of God are the children of God.

The Spirit you received does not make you slaves, so that you live in fear again; rather, the Spirit you received brought about your adoption to sonship. And by him we cry, "Abba, Father."

The Spirit himself testifies with our spirit that we are God's children. — Romans 8:14-16

In the same way, the Spirit helps us in our weakness. We do not know what we ought to pray for, but the Spirit himself intercedes for us through wordless groans.

And he who searches our hearts knows the mind of the Spirit, because the Spirit intercedes for God's people in accordance with the will of God. — Romans 8:26-27 (Emphasis added.)

We need the Holy Spirit to intercede because we do not know what we ought to pray. This act of surrender is extremely freeing and empowering. Stanley Jones writes:

Prayer is surrender to the will of God and cooperation with that will. If I throw out a boat hook from the boat and catch hold of the shore and pull, do I pull the shore to me, or do I pull myself to the shore? Prayer is not pulling God to my will, but the aligning of my will to the will of God. [3]

Gordon T. Smith refers to this as listening prayer:

[Prayer] needs to be listening prayer. For so many, prayer is talking to God rather than communion with God ... Discerning prayer requires that at times we simply shut up and remain silent in the presence of God.[4]

Too often believers are too busy telling God what should transpire rather than being inspired by the Holy Spirit. During this time of listening the Spirit gives us the words to pray—sometimes in tongues, but usually not.

Our prayer group sometimes receives information about a particular person or situation needing prayer. We usually share a Scripture verse at this time as the Spirit guides. To be in tune to God's Word during prayer is of the utmost importance. "Holy Scripture is the starting point and measuring rod for individual [and group] insight."[5]

If we want to hear the voice of Jesus, then we must be in God's Word. Gordon T. Smith contends,

The Spirit will never contradict Scripture. When we are faced with competing options, both or all of which may be good and valid options, what we will long for is communion with Christ by His Spirit. So if we have neglected the study of Scripture, we will be at a distinct disadvantage.[6]

God keeps his Word. We must be people of the Word!

All of our prayer warriors are involved in Bible reading and/or Bible study. As we are guided by the Holy Spirit in prayer, then, as Edwin Keith writes, "*Prayer is exhaling the spirit of man and inhaling the spirit of God*."[7] (Emphasis added.)

...That Leads to Transformation

> ***Those who look to him are radiant; their faces are never covered with shame.***
>
> **— Psalm 34:5**

We are changed. We are transformed when we pray. It is impossible to enter the presence of King Jesus and remain the same as before the encounter. Paul writes,

> ***The Son* [Jesus] *is the image of the invisible God, the firstborn over all creation.***
>
> ***For in him all things were created: things in heaven and on earth, visible and invisible, whether thrones or powers or rulers or authorities; all things have been created through him and for him.***
>
> ***He is before all things, and in him all things hold together.***
>
> *And he is the head of the body, the church; he is the beginning and the firstborn from among the dead, so that in everything he might have the supremacy*.
>
> ***For God was pleased to have all his fullness dwell in him,***
>
> ***and through him to reconcile to himself all things, whether things on earth or things in heaven, by making peace through his blood, shed on the cross.***

Once you were alienated from God and were enemies in your minds because of your evil behavior.

But now he has reconciled you by Christ's physical body through death to present you holy in his sight, without blemish and free from accusation—

— Colossians 1:15-22 (Emphasis added.)

How can we remain the same when we enter into the presence of the King of Kings? Imagine entering Almighty God's throne room and having the privilege of addressing the King as "Daddy." How can this ever be boring? People get excited when they meet the president of the United States, a sports figure or a movie star, and they will even pay thousands of dollars to meet such people. After the description of Jesus in Colossians, how can we not be excited and changed by an audience with Him? Is it any wonder that those who are the most peaceful and patient people in our congregations are those who pray frequently?

Many years ago I was on the stewardship committee in our local congregation when we were starting a building program. I presented the need for offerings above our tithes in order to start the building project. Stan, one of the senior saints and a prayer warrior, responded by saying, "I am on a fixed income. How can I possibly give any more?" But before I even had time to reply, Stan's tone changed and he quietly said, "I'm sorry, we will pray and God will provide." This is the change that being in King Jesus' presence can make.

Every Monday evening I see a remarkable change in myself and others at our prayer meetings. People come to the prayer meetings tired, angry, frustrated, hurting or depressed, but by the time we leave the meeting we are at peace and usually joyful.

One time Darol, one of our prayer warriors, was angry when he came because his neighbor had been playing Latino music so loud Darol could hear it in his house. When Darol arrived at Amazing Grace for prayer, we were playing some Latino praise music loudly at the beginning of prayer. Darol humbly shared that evening that God had given him a message. He came into the presence of the King angry, and left at peace and changed.

We cannot enter the presence of King Jesus and not be changed. Christianity without transformation is a cheap imitation. Prayer is so much more than a reverent petition to a deity. Get excited, because in prayer we are going to see the King!

DISCUSSION OR REFLECTION QUESTIONS:

1. What was your opinion and definition of prayer before you read this chapter? How has your opinion changed?

2. Do you spend time in listening prayer?

3. Have you heard or experienced the voice of God?

4. Romans 8:26-27 is often used to support the gift of tongues. Do you believe this is a legitimate interpretation of this text?

5. Do you employ your emotions as well as your reason in prayer? Why or why not?

Chapter Three

The Power of Prayer

There are six main points I wish to address in this chapter pertaining to the power of prayer:

- Power in the Presence,
- Prayer and Prophecy,
- Prayer and Justice,
- Changes Wrought by Prayer,
- Prayer and Personal Transformation, and
- Power of Communal Prayer.

I realize there are many other facets to the power God unleashes in prayer, but these six come from my experience with God's power in the presence of the King and from my study of the following text:

> *Then the LORD said to Moses, "Leave this place, you and the people you brought up out of Egypt, and go up to the land I promised on oath to Abraham, Isaac and Jacob, saying, 'I will give it to your descendants.'*

I will send an angel before you and drive out the Canaanites, Amorites, Hittites, Perizzites, Hivites and Jebusites.

Go up to the land flowing with milk and honey. But I will not go with you, because you are a stiff-necked people and I might destroy you on the way."

When the people heard these distressing words, they began to mourn and no one put on any ornaments.

For the LORD had said to Moses, "Tell the Israelites, 'You are a stiff-necked people. If I were to go with you even for a moment, I might destroy you. Now take off your ornaments and I will decide what to do with you.'"

So the Israelites stripped off their ornaments at Mount Horeb.

Now Moses used to take a tent and pitch it outside the camp some distance away, calling it the "tent of meeting." Anyone inquiring of the LORD would go to the tent of meeting outside the camp.

And whenever Moses went out to the tent, all the people rose and stood at the entrances to their tents, watching Moses until he entered the tent.

As Moses went into the tent, the pillar of cloud would come down and stay at the entrance, while the LORD spoke with Moses.

Whenever the people saw the pillar of cloud standing at the entrance to the tent, they all stood and worshiped, each at the entrance to his tent.

The LORD would speak to Moses face to face, as a man speaks with his friend. Then Moses would return to the camp, but his young aide Joshua son of Nun did not leave the tent.

Moses said to the Lord, *"You have been telling me, 'Lead these people,' but you have not let me know whom you will send with me. You have said, 'I know you by name and you have found favor with me.'*

If you are pleased with me, teach me your ways so I may know you and continue to find favor with you. Remember that this nation is your people."

The Lord *replied, "My Presence will go with you, and I will give you rest."*

Then Moses said to him, "If your Presence does not go with us, do not send us up from here.

How will anyone know that you are pleased with me and with your people unless you go with us? What else will distinguish me and your people from all the other people on the face of the earth?"

And the Lord *said to Moses, "I will do the very thing you have asked, because I am pleased with you and I know you by name."*

— Exodus 33:1-17

Power in the Presence

After reading this text, it is a good time to review my definition of prayer:

> Prayer is seeking the Lord, entering His presence through Jesus Christ, and having a heart to heart conversation with God guided by the Holy Spirit that leads to transformation.

In other words, we seek an audience with the King, *Yahweh*. We receive the audience and enter into the King's presence through the blood of Jesus. We are now in the presence of almighty God, the King of kings and

Lord of lords. This is the essence of prayer. This is where the power of prayer comes from. **The power in prayer is power in God's presence.** In the presence of God we experience the ultimate source of power in heaven and earth as described in 1 Chronicles:

> *Yours, O Lord, is the greatness and the power and the glory and the majesty and the splendor, for everything in heaven and earth is yours. Yours, O Lord, is the kingdom; you are exalted as head over all.* — 1 Chronicles 29:11

Power in the presence of God is demonstrated by Moses in Exodus 33:15:

> *Then Moses said to him, "**If your Presence does not go with us, do not send us up from here.***
>
> ***How will anyone know that you are pleased with me and with your people unless you go with us?** What else will distinguish me and your people from all the other people on the face of the earth?"* (Emphasis added.)

Moses realized that without God's presence, he and his people would be powerless to defeat the people who occupied the Promised Land. The Chosen people knew they could not go it alone. They would be the same as the people who live their lives without God—empty, weak, hopeless and powerless.

The importance of God's presence is also proclaimed by King David in the psalms:

> *Blessed are those who have learned to acclaim you, who walk in the light of your presence, O Lord."* — Psalm 89:15

"Do not cast me from your presence or take your Holy Spirit from me." — Psalm 51:11

Prayer is more about being in the presence of God than about what we do or say. There is power being in the presence of the King. Mother Teresa illustrated this point. Dan Rather, CBS news anchor, once asked Mother Teresa what she said during her prayers. She answered, "I listen."

Rather then asked, "Well, then, what does God say?"

To that Mother Teresa smiled with confidence and answered, "He listens."[8] Mother Teresa realized prayer is simply being in God's presence.

We receive power by being in the presence of King Jesus. There are times on Monday evenings at our prayer meeting when we lay on hands and pray for others. At these times we often feel the power of God passing through us and entering the people we're praying for, and they acknowledge receiving power from our touch. The power does not come from us. The power comes from the King in whose presence we pray.

Prayer and Prophecy

As Moses went into the tent, the pillar of cloud would come down and stay at the entrance while the Lord spoke with Moses. Whenever the people saw the pillar of cloud standing at the entrance to the tent, they all stood and worshiped, each at the entrance to his tent. The Lord spoke to Moses face to face, as a man speaks with his friend. Then Moses would return to the camp, but his young aide Joshua, son of Nun, did not leave the tent (Exodus 33:9-11). Moses spoke to God face to face, and then returned with a word from the Lord. This still happens today and it is called prophecy. Prophecy is receiving a Word from God. It can be a present truth revealed in God's Word or a future reality. Here are some examples of God's present truth spoken in the Bible:

Salt and Light:

> *You are the salt of the earth. But if the salt loses its saltiness, how can it be made salty again? It is no longer good for anything, except to be thrown out and trampled by men.*
>
> *You are the light of the world. A city on a hill cannot be hidden.* — Matthew 5:13-14

Murder:

> *You have heard that it was said to the people long ago, "Do not murder, and anyone who murders will be subject to judgment."*
>
> *But I tell you that anyone who is angry with his brother will be subject to judgment. Again, anyone who says to his brother, "Raca," is answerable to the Sanhedrin. But anyone who says, "You fool!'" will be in danger of the fire of hell.*
>
> — Matthew 5:21-22

Adultery

> *You have heard that it was said, "Do not commit adultery.'"*
>
> *But I tell you that anyone who looks at a woman lustfully has already committed adultery with her in his heart.* — Matthew 5:27-28

Now these are prophetic words spoken by Jesus that talk of a present reality. However, prophecy can also speak of a future reality. The Lord speaks to us in prayer, visions, and dreams about events that will occur in the future. Here are a couple of examples from the book of Acts.

> *After we had been there a number of days, a prophet named Agabus came down from Judea.*

Coming over to us, he took Paul's belt, tied his own hands and feet with it and said, "The Holy Spirit says, 'In this way the Jews of Jerusalem will bind the owner of this belt and will hand him over to the Gentiles.'" — Acts 21:10-11

Paul went to Jerusalem despite this prophecy and ended up being handed over to the Romans. Eventually he was sent to Rome to stand before the emperor. Agabus was proven to be a true prophet because his prophecy was fulfilled. However, this prophecy was not created by Agabus—the Holy Spirit made it known to him, as is the case of all prophecy.

The next example from the book of Acts involves Peter and Cornelius, a Roman soldier.

About noon the following day as they were on their journey and approaching the city, Peter went up on the roof to pray.

He became hungry and wanted something to eat, and while the meal was being prepared, he fell into a trance.

He saw heaven opened and something like a large sheet being let down to earth by its four corners.

It contained all kinds of four-footed animals, as well as reptiles of the earth and birds of the air.

Then a voice told him, "Get up, Peter. Kill and eat."

"Surely not, Lord!" Peter replied. "I have never eaten anything impure or unclean."

The voice spoke to him a second time, "Do not call anything impure that God has made clean."

This happened three times, and immediately the sheet was taken back to heaven.

While Peter was wondering about the meaning of the vision, the men sent by Cornelius found out where Simon's house was and stopped at the gate.

They called out, asking if Simon who was known as Peter was staying there.

While Peter was still thinking about the vision, the Spirit said to him, "Simon, three men are looking for you.

So get up and go downstairs. Do not hesitate to go with them, for I have sent them."

Peter went down and said to the men, "I'm the one you're looking for. Why have you come?"

The men replied, "We have come from Cornelius the centurion. He is a righteous and God-fearing man, who is respected by all the Jewish people. A holy angel told him to have you come to his house so that he could hear what you have to say."

Then Peter invited the men into the house to be his guests. — Acts 10:9-13

In this account Peter is directed by the Holy Spirit in a vision and Cornelius is led by an angel (messenger of God). Once again the prophecy comes true because the foretold event occurs.

Prophecy—the foretelling of future events—still happens today. Recently, there was a woman who formerly served many years in prison for methamphetamine use, but who had not used the drug for over four years. However, she continued to drink alcohol. I warned her on many occasions, personally and in my sermons, that she was playing with fire. She refused to heed my warnings.

One day during my devotions the Lord made it clear that she would end up in jail with a DUI if she persisted in this behavior. I knew it was going to happen soon. I shared with my brother, Pastor Perry, that she would end up getting a DUI and being incarcerated. I also warned her again, which resulted in an argument. Two weeks later she was arrested for DUI and served time in jail. This was a prophecy fulfilled. It was not my idea. It was not fulfilled by me, but by Jesus Christ. In prayer we can receive a word from God.

Another example of prophecy took place in my life around 1990. I was working as a sales manager during the day and attending Fuller Seminary at night. During this time I would pray at work in my car at lunch time with a friend who was attending another Christian church. During one of these prayer sessions my friend shared that his wife had a dream of me preaching in a desert. She described my preaching as water flowing into this desert.

At the time, we were experimenting with a house church in our home in Nuevo, California. My friend asked if it was a desert in Nuevo. I replied it was rocky, very hot and similar to a desert. I thought for sure this dream applied to my current circumstance. I was wrong. This prophecy was fulfilled in 1996 when I was called to a church in Phoenix, Arizona. At the time of this sister's dream, my wife and I had no plans whatsoever to move to Phoenix. I believe this was an example of a prophetic dream that was fulfilled years later.

One more example of prophecy occurred recently when our treasurer, Liz Parker, called me early one morning. She was distraught over a dream she'd had that night. In the dream someone very dear to the church died, and she believed we needed to pray in order to save their life. We commenced praying, and no one died. However, one of our members who had relapsed on meth was arrested for possession of dangerous drugs and drug paraphernalia (syringes, needles). Months later when we went to court with this brother, Liz told me that this brother was the one who she was warned about in her dream. He was the man we were praying for and God in His mercy spared his life. God still speaks to His people in prayer, visions and dreams.

Prayer and Justice

> *Moses said to the Lord, "You have been telling me, 'Lead these people,' but you have not let me know whom you will send with me. You have said, 'I know you by name and you have found favor with me.'*
>
> *If you are pleased with me, teach me your ways so I may know you and continue to find favor with you. Remember that this nation is your people."*
>
> ***The Lord replied, "My Presence will go with you, and I will give you rest."*** (Emphasis added.) — Exodus 33:12-14

Moses prayed for justice, and the Lord had mercy and demonstrated His justice. We expect to receive justice when we pray in God's presence. Why? Simply because God is always just. The following Scriptures declare God's justice:

> *The Lord within her is righteous; he does no wrong. Morning by morning he dispenses his justice, and every new day he does not fail, yet the unrighteous know no shame.*
>
> — Zephaniah 3:5

> *For the Lord is righteous, he loves justice; upright men will see his face.* — Psalm 11:7

> *The Lord loves righteousness and justice; the earth is full of his unfailing love.* — Psalm 33:5

It is a tremendous comfort to know that Our King deals justly with us. The Lord—who created all people and things and knows all people and things intimately—is uniquely qualified to dispense justice in its purest form. God dispenses His justice impartially in Spirit, righteousness, and truth.

Since you call on a Father who judges each man's work impartially, live your lives as strangers here in reverent fear. — 1 Peter 1:17

When they hurled their insults at him, he did not retaliate; when he suffered, he made no threats. Instead, he entrusted himself to him who judges justly. — 1 Peter 2:23

And I will ask the Father, and he will give you another Counselor to be with you forever—

the Spirit of truth. The world cannot accept him, because it neither sees him nor knows him. But you know him, for he lives with you and will be in you.

I will not leave you as orphans; I will come to you. — John 14:16-18

This is the one who came by water and blood—Jesus Christ. He did not come by water only, but by water and blood. And it is the Spirit who testifies, because the Spirit is the truth.

— 1 John 5:6

He will judge the world in righteousness; he will govern the peoples with justice. — Psalm 9:8

Let them sing before the Lord, for he comes to judge the earth. He will judge the world in righteousness and the peoples with equity.

— Psalm 98:9

Jesus answered, "Even if I testify on my own behalf, my testimony is valid, for I know where I came from and where I am going. But you have no idea where I come from or where I am going.

You judge by human standards; I pass judgment on no one.

But if I do judge, my decisions are right, because I am not alone. I stand with the Father, who sent me. — John 8:14-16

And the LORD said, "Listen to what the unjust judge says.

And will not God bring about justice for his chosen ones, who cry out to him day and night? Will he keep putting them off?

I tell you, he will see that they get justice, and quickly. However, when the Son of Man comes, will he find faith on the earth?" — Luke 18:6-8

We know when we pray to our Father we will receive justice. Our King is truth, all-just, all-knowing and righteous. What a comfort it is to know our prayers are not heard by an arbitrary judge! When we converse with our God, He listens. He knows every detail surrounding our situation, and judges us and our situation in Spirit and truth.

A great example of this is Daniel, who was thrown into the lion's den by King Darius of Persia for refusing to stop praying to *Yahweh*, the one true God. At first glance, getting thrown into a lion's den seems very unjust. Daniel could have complained to God about allowing this to happen.

However, Daniel responded in trust in God's justice, and in prayer to God. Ultimately, Daniel was miraculously saved from the lions, "*And when Daniel was lifted from the den, no wound was found on him, because he had trusted in his God"* (Daniel 6:23).

At the same time, Daniel's enemies—who sought his destruction—were promptly thrown into the lion's den, and were devoured by the lions. *Yahweh's* justice reigns.

In response, the Lord expects us to be a just people. When we discern a situation, we should judge in Spirit and truth. The Scriptures declare:

> *For the LORD is righteous, he loves justice; upright men will see his face.* — Psalm 11:7

> *The LORD loves righteousness and justice; the earth is full of his unfailing love.* — Psalm 33:5

> *Evil men do not understand justice, but those who seek the LORD understand it* [justice] *fully.*
> — Proverbs 28:5

> *But you must return to your God; maintain love and justice, and wait for your God always.*
> — Hosea 12:6

> *They devour widows' houses and for a show make lengthy prayers. Such men will be punished most severely."* — Luke 20:47

> *This is what the LORD says: Do what is just and right. Rescue from the hand of his oppressor the one who has been robbed. Do no wrong or violence to the alien, the fatherless or the widow, and do not shed innocent blood in this place.*
> — Jeremiah 22:3

The Scriptures are clear: we are to be people who love justice and pray for justice. God requires a response from His people when they receive justice. God's children are to be a justice-loving, a justice-praying, and a justice-doing people. The Scriptures, the Word of God, are very emphatic regarding justice. If we want and pray for justice for ourselves, how much more should we pray for and desire justice for others?

Changes Wrought by Prayer

> *When the people heard these distressing words,* ***they began to mourn and no one put on any ornaments****.*
>
> *For the LORD had said to Moses, "Tell the Israelites, 'You are a stiff-necked people. If I were to go with you even for a moment, I might destroy you. Now take off your ornaments and I will decide what to do with you.'"*
>
> ***So the Israelites stripped off their ornaments at Mount Horeb.*** (Emphasis added.)
>
> — Exodus 33:4-6

The people heard of the Lord's rejection of Israel given to Moses in prayer, so they mourned, removed their ornaments, and repented. Later the Lord changed His mind and promised Moses that He, the Lord God, would go with Moses and the chosen people and give them rest in the Promised Land. Prayer changed the people, it changed Moses, and it changed the Lord's decision.

The Lord answers our prayers for situations and people. Here are some of the numerous examples in the Scriptures of the power of prayer:

> *Isaac prayed to the LORD on behalf of his wife, because she was barren. The LORD answered his prayer, and his wife Rebekah became pregnant.*
>
> — Genesis 25:21

> *David built an altar to the LORD there and sacrificed burnt offerings and fellowship offerings. Then the*

Lord answered prayer in behalf of the land, and the plague on Israel was stopped.
— 2 Samuel 24:25

Go back and tell Hezekiah, the leader of my people, "This is what the Lord, the God of your father David, says: I have heard your prayer and seen your tears; I will heal you. On the third day from now you will go up to the temple of the Lord." — 2 Kings 20:5

Go and tell Hezekiah, "This is what the Lord, the God of your father David, says: I have heard your prayer and seen your tears; I will add fifteen years to your life." — Isaiah 38:5

If you believe, you will receive whatever you ask for in prayer." — Matthew 21:22

He replied, "This kind can come out only by prayer." — Mark 9:29

His father was sick in bed, suffering from fever and dysentery. Paul went in to see him and, after prayer, placed his hands on him and healed him.
— Acts 28:8

Finally, brothers, pray for us that the message of the Lord may spread rapidly and be honored, just as it was with you. — 2 Thessalonians 3:1

And the prayer offered in faith will make the sick person well; the Lord will raise him up. If he has sinned, he will be forgiven. — James 5:15

Prayer changes people, their lives and their circumstances. Many years ago, an x-ray showed that Mary, one of our jail pastors, had a very large lump (2 inches in diameter) on her breast. The doctor was alarmed and told Mary it appeared to be cancerous. The doctor ordered a sonogram-type exam immediately. As Mary was lying on the table waiting for the nurse to come in, she prayed that God would remove the cancer/tumor from her body. She boldly claimed healing in Jesus name.

When the young nurse came in for the exam, she could not find the lump that appeared on the x-ray. The young nurse called in her nursing supervisor while Mary continued praying in silence.

The nursing supervisor also could not find the cancer. She called in the doctor. The doctor and nurses examined Mary for over two hours and found nothing. The evidence on the x-ray clearly pointed to a malignant tumor that Mary, the doctor and nurses had previously felt.

The doctor and nurses were completely stumped. The tumor was gone. Mary told them God had healed her. After two hours of intense examination, the doctor declared the lump was gone and released Mary. She has been cancer-free since.

To the unbeliever this would be called a coincidence or a misdiagnosis. To Mary and other believers, it is the hand of God. Personally, I have seen so many cases of "misdiagnosis" that the doctors today are either completely incompetent or the Kingdom of God is among us. I choose to believe the latter. In the Kingdom of God even death can be overthrown.

Approximately ten years ago, I received a call from the local hospital chaplain as I was preparing for a Wednesday evening service. He needed a Lutheran pastor to come and baptize a woman who was terminally ill. The woman was ventilated in ICU and unconscious. The doctor said she had a two percent chance of living, and expected her to die before the day was over. When a doctor says you have a two percent chance of living, you are as good as dead.

I went to the hospital and saw the 39-year-old woman surrounded by her family. The woman was an alcoholic and was suffering liver failure. To say she was jaundiced would be an understatement. She was literally yellow. I had never seen anyone that jaundiced, and to this day I have never seen any other patient whose skin was so yellow.

Even though the woman was unconscious, I baptized her and then held her hand as I led the family in prayer. I left feeling the presence of the Lord but thought that she would be dead by morning.

The following Monday I called the chaplain, expecting to be asked to preach at her funeral. The chaplain was excited and told me that the woman was going home that very day with her family. She was alive, alert, and healed. The chaplain went on to say that the healing started right after I left the hospital.

I believe the Lord Jesus healed this woman—and obviously, it was not on account of my faith, the family's faith or the woman's faith. We all thought she was as good as dead—that is why she was baptized. To this day, I believe this woman was raised from the jaws of death, just so I could tell her story to the glory of Jesus.

Finally, in regard to exorcism—the expulsion of demons from people—I believe demons still exist and that they possess people. Jesus believed there were demons and drove them out of many people. I am not going to question Jesus' authority.

> *Moreover, demons came out of many people, shouting, "You are the Son of God!" But he [Jesus] rebuked them and would not allow them to speak, because they knew he was the Christ.*
>
> — Luke 4:41

> *When Jesus had called the Twelve together, he gave them power and authority to drive out all demons and to cure diseases,* — Luke 9:1

Somehow in our postmodern culture we have become too sophisticated for demons, and that is exactly what they want. C. S. Lewis writes,

> There are two equal and opposite errors into which our race can fall about the devils. **One is to disbelieve their existence. The other is to believe, and to feel an excessive and unhealthy interest in them. They themselves are equally pleased by both errors and hail a materialist or a magician with the same delight.**[9] (Emphasis added.)

I am not a magician and don't believe in looking for demons under every bush, but there are times when we cannot be naïve about their existence or their desire to halt the mission of the church. **Satan usually uses people to do his dirty work.** In my last eight years at Amazing Grace, on more than one occasion I have witnessed members of the church who have had an unusually and continually critical spirit, a demon.

On Mondays, we pray against the demons. We do not pray against the person. Usually, the demon leaves the person or the person leaves the church. It happens both ways, but when a person leaves the church I continue to pray for them.

When a person leaves the church, pastors have been trained to see this as a loss and believe me, we all suffer the sense of loss when someone departs Amazing Grace, especially Pastor Perry and me. But the spiritual health and well-being of the church are more important than our feelings. Generally, these people who leave the church are very religious but not very connected to Jesus. If you recall, Jesus' problems were caused by some very religious people who were not living in a personal relation with Jesus or His Father. John writes:

> *Why is my language not clear to you? Because you are unable to hear what I say.*
>
> *You belong to your father, the devil, and you want to carry out your father's desire. He was a murderer from the beginning, not holding to the truth, for there is no truth in him. When he lies, he speaks his native language, for he is a liar and the father of lies.*
>
> *Yet because I tell the truth, you do not believe me!* — John 8:43-45

I realize these are hard words, but we do not want to be soft on Satan and his demons who love to destroy churches. Friends, we cannot afford to be politically correct regarding spiritual warfare. Paul writes:

> ***For our struggle is not against flesh and blood, but against the rulers, against the authorities, against the powers of this dark world and against the spiritual forces of evil in the heavenly realms.*** — Ephesians 6:12 (Emphasis added.)

We fight against demons and not people with our prayers!

PRAYER AND PERSONAL TRANSFORMATION

> *If you are pleased with me,* ***teach me your ways so I may know you and continue to find favor with you.*** *Remember that this nation is your people."* — Exodus 33:13 (Emphasis added.)

After Moses prayed, his face was aglow and radiant because he had been in the presence of *Yahweh*. Moses was changed by being in the presence of God. This is still true today for believers who pray in the presence of King Jesus. Paul describes this to the church at Corinth:

> *Whenever, though, they turn to face God as Moses did, God removes the veil and there they are—face-to-face! They suddenly recognize that God is a living, personal presence, not a piece of chiseled stone. And when God is personally present, a living Spirit, that old, constricting legislation is recognized as obsolete. We're free of it! All of us! Nothing between us and God, our faces shining with the brightness of his face. And so we are transfigured much like the Messiah, our lives gradually becoming brighter and more beautiful as God enters our lives and we become like him.*
>
> — 2 Corinthians 3:16-18 (*The Message*)

Ultimately, we enter the throne room of Grace in order to be in the presence of King Jesus, and in His presence we are changed. C. S. Lewis, the great Christian apologist, discussed in *A Grief Observed* how he responded to a friend when asked about how his prayers were going for his wife, Joy, who was dying from cancer. Lewis said very good, and his friend assumed Joy's condition had improved and talked of the power of prayer. Lewis stopped him by saying,

> That's not why I pray, Harry, I pray because I can't help myself. I pray because I'm helpless. I pray because the need flows out of me all the time, waking and sleeping. It doesn't change God; it changes me.[10]

Prayer changes us. When we first started our prayer meetings on Monday evening, Pastor Perry and I prayed—expecting God to grow and change our church. Well, our church did grow and it did change, but the greatest changes happened in us. We started to love Mondays for the experience of God's presence. We found that through the presence of Jesus we were empowered to do more than we ever imagined for the Kingdom of God. The things we discovered ourselves doing were completely unplanned by us, and generally the process went very smoothly in accomplishing the task.

In the past two years, our preaching has improved dramatically because of the anointing of the Holy Spirit. I always thought that the whole "anointed preacher" thing was a bunch of bunk, until I experienced it personally. Then, I found myself caught up with a sense of urgency and a need for people to listen and understand what I was saying. I became more animated, especially at our Spanish worship, and I was moving and gesturing with authority. At times when I preach, I feel as if my hair is on fire.

Pastor Perry has experienced the same phenomenon in his preaching, but he feels a warm hand touching his back while he preaches. Perry literally stomps, points and shouts now while preaching. This is even more amazing when you consider that for 25 years, he was a very conservative Missouri Synod Lutheran pastor.

There ***is*** such a thing as anointed preaching, and it is a pure gift from the Holy Spirit. Perry and I would be the first to admit, "It ain't us!" Our sermons go longer—and no one complains. In fact, the people have actually asked for more preaching. I have preached a 45-minute sermon, which is way outside the box for me. For many years, my sermons were 15 minutes or less. But the response of the congregation is the greatest surprise; they love it and are being changed into disciples of Jesus. This is just one of the changes God has wrought in us.

The other change is that the importance of numbers—nickels and noses—has diminished. What is of ultimate importance to us now is the presence of God. In our prayers, worship, preaching, teaching and lives, we simply want to live in the kingdom of God, in the presence of King Jesus.

Power of Communal Prayer

Prayer is essential in every mission field. Walter C. Hobbs, in his chapter titled "Dependence on the Holy Spirit" in *Treasures in Clay Jars*, writes,

> Missional churches know that trouble will surely batter them; indecision will plague them; evil will terrorize them ... The early churches knew this well (Acts 21:5), and just in case they might forget it they were often reminded by the apostles (see 1 Thessalonians 5:17). Prayer was essential to the people of God in their mission of carrying Good News to the nations. It still is. The missional church is incapable of fulfilling its call, save for guidance from the Holy Spirit of God and for the Spirit's empowerment of the church's witness to that reality.[11]

Without the power of the Holy Spirit through prayer, the Church is simply an empty vessel. Prayer paves the way for mission and ministry. It is essential to start everything with prayer. Jonathan Edwards stated,

> Before God has something very great to accomplish for His Church, it is His will that there should precede it the fervent prayers of His people."[12]

The birthing of a vision for the church out of prayer is a two-pronged approach. It involves both the personal prayer life and focus as a pastor as well as the corporate prayer life and focus in the church.

The pastor's personal prayer life needs to focus more on the harvest and listening to God, rather than doing all the speaking. There also has to be an emphasis and opportunity for the members of the church to enter the trenches and pray.

The need for prayer in all churches is immense, but at Amazing Grace prayer is mandatory for our life. Amazing Grace is unique in that it is an urban congregation that reaches out to people other churches generally would not seek. These include: the incarcerated and their families; noisy, undisciplined children; illegal aliens; Spanish-speaking people; convicted felons; the mentally disabled; divorced persons; addicts and recovering addicts; unmarried cohabitating couples; and the poor. Not all churches ignore this mission field, but many suburban churches seek middle-class families.

There are five main opportunities for life giving prayer at Amazing Grace: the prayer chain, the daily prayer warriors, the Monday prayer meeting, the jail churches, and the prayers of the church at worship.

The church has a prayer chain of approximately 100 members for immediate prayer requests. These prayer warriors are contacted by email. The members of our church simply call our prayer chain coordinator with their requests, and he sends them out by email. It is interesting to note that we receive many prayer requests from unchurched friends and from acquaintances of members. Although these people won't attend a church and may have negative feelings about Christianity—when troubles arise, they reach out to the "God-people" in their lives.

And we pray for them, no questions asked.

We also employ a list of approximately 110 daily prayer warriors. Each is assigned a specific day of the month and given a prayer chart to post in their homes. I recommend posting the charts on the refrigerator, bathroom mirror or any place where they can be viewed daily.

For example, Fred may be assigned the third day of the month. This means that on the third of every month everyone else on the prayer chart will pray for Fred and his family, as well as for the church, the jail churches, the pastors and their families, and the jail pastors and their families. At the same time, Fred prays daily for the church, the jail churches, the pastors and their families, the jail pastors and their families, and for other members assigned to that particular day.

This vital ministry always needs to be updated, and the focus of the harvest and visioning needs to be reinforced in the prayers. There is tremendous power in this simple prayer chart and it changes people and events in the church. I know of one woman who always tries to schedule important events on her prayer day so that she knows she is covered by the prayers of others.

I have already discussed our prayer meetings on Monday evenings in the Introduction. Of all the prayer opportunities at Amazing Grace, I have discovered this to be the most spiritually powerful and life-changing.

Yes, people and events have been changed by our prayer meetings, but most importantly the Spirit has changed me and continues to change me through these prayer times. Our Monday prayer meetings have enriched our members, our worship, and our pastors. I must restate—numbers are not important. Pastors, you need to be willing to pray, even if you are the only one there. You will be blessed.

Another extremely powerful prayer opportunity comes from our jail churches. The main connection between the mother church and the jail churches is the prayer request cards written by the inmates. At the beginning of each jail service, note cards and pencils are distributed to the inmates. The inmates write their first name and their prayer requests on the cards. The requests consist of prayers for family—their wives, husbands, girlfriends, children, grandchildren and parents—and for court appearances.

As the inmates mature, however, the prayer requests are for faith for themselves, the other inmates, their families and others. They also often ask for prayer for their jail pastors. All of these prayer requests are then collected and prayed over by the jail pastors. The following Sunday at worship, they are distributed to the members of the mother church. Some prayer requests are in Spanish and some in English. The members take the cards home and pray daily for the inmates for one week or longer, depending on the member who receives them.

These prayer requests have formed a tremendous bond between the inmates and the mother church. These two very different groups of people come to know each other before the throne of God in prayer before they ever have a chance to meet. When the inmates are released and visit the mother church, they see the saints who have been upholding them in prayer. At the same time, the members see the saints they have been praying for behind jail bars. It is a very holy time.

One memorable meeting was the first time Amazing Grace member Hazel met former inmate Joshua at a Sunday service at Amazing Grace. The first thing Hazel said was, "Joshua, you are the one I have been praying for." Joshua grinned from ear to ear and gave Hazel a hug. These meetings are joyous occasions.

Furthermore, both the inmates and members of the mother church experience the power of prayer. For example, jail Pastor Paul shared a praise in Amazing Grace's Sunday worship—one inmate was facing a minimum of 14 years in prison, and there was no way he could receive a more lenient sentence. After sending in numerous prayer requests to the mother church, however, this inmate received only a six-month probation. Amazing Grace and this inmate witnessed the power of prayer firsthand. This type of praise report has become a common occurrence in the churches. The prayers outside the jails are a powerful spiritual force.

Inside the jails, the mother church and jail churches receive additional prayer cover. The jail pastors ask the inmates to pray for personal prayer requests and for prayer requests from the mother church. Dr. Bob Logan describes the power of this vulnerability:

> *Intercession is a heavy burden. When leaders allow themselves to need the support of others and be cared for in prayer, they become a more connected part of the whole body of Christ.*[13]

When the jail pastor returns the following week for worship, the inmates always ask for updates to the prayer requests. It makes the inmates feel connected and important to the body of Christ. Their faith regarding prayer is fresh and childlike. It is clear to all that the inmates' prayers are very powerful and effective. In response to their prayers, marriages have healed, cancer has been cured and addicts have entered recovery. It is amazing that inmates locked in cages can focus on others outside the jails and pray for them and their churches. This is a very holy and profound experience.

Our final prayer opportunity is during worship on Sundays or Wednesday evenings. Most churches have a time for the petitions of the people during worship. Many times this is a very guarded, short or exclusive time of prayer. It can be exclusive in that only one person prays or the same people always pray. At Amazing Grace, although the pastors lead the petitions, the members all feel free to pray their petitions aloud.

This is an evolving process, with more people praying—and praying more boldly and longer about intimate happenings and people in their lives. It has evolved with our entire emphasis on prayer, and it also is making Amazing Grace a safe place. A place where people can share their lives and stories without having to worry about them becoming a source of gossip or degradation. The church must be a safe place for all things, but especially for prayer.

DISCUSSION OR REFLECTION QUESTIONS:

1. How do you experience the presence of God in prayer?

2. Do you thirst for the presence of God? Read Psalm 63:1-8 and discuss.

3. Have you experienced power in your prayers? Please describe.

4. Have you experienced a true prophecy? Please describe.

5. Is prophecy for today or a gift for the 1st century church only? Discuss Acts 2:16-18.

6. Do you feel your church is a safe place to pray? Why or why not?

7. What opportunities are provided for prayer in your church? What opportunities would you like to see added? Discuss Acts 2: 42-43.

Chapter Four

How To Pray

Whenever someone asks me how they can learn to pray, I always send them to the Psalter. It is in the Psalms where we see how God's people have prayed to Him for over 3,000 years. David, who authored many of the Psalms, has provided us a great model for prayer in all the Psalms—but particularly in Psalm 51:

> For the director of music. A psalm of David. When the prophet Nathan came to him after David had committed adultery with Bathsheba.
>
> *Have mercy on me, O God, according to your unfailing love; according to your great compassion blot out my transgressions. Wash away all my iniquity and cleanse me from my sin.*
>
> *For I know my transgressions, and my sin is always before me.*
>
> *Against you, you only, have I sinned and done what is evil in your sight, so that you are proved right when you speak and justified when you judge.*

Surely I was sinful at birth, sinful from the time my mother conceived me.

Surely you desire truth in the inner parts; you teach me wisdom in the inmost place.

Cleanse me with hyssop, and I will be clean; wash me, and I will be whiter than snow.

Let me hear joy and gladness; let the bones you have crushed rejoice.

Hide your face from my sins and blot out all my iniquity.

Create in me a pure heart, O God, and renew a steadfast spirit within me.

Do not cast me from your presence or take your Holy Spirit from me.

Restore to me the joy of your salvation and grant me a willing spirit, to sustain me.

I'll demonstrate the "how to pray" model from how we pray on Monday evenings and weave Psalm 51 and other psalms into the process.

The foremost step in prayer is entering the presence of the King. Set a time and a quiet place to enter or realize the presence of the living God. The Lord commands this in Psalm 46:10, "*Be still, and know that I am God; I will be exalted among the nations, I will be exalted in the earth*." Don't worry about talking to God. He is not far away—acknowledge God's presence. On Monday evenings we spend 20-60 minutes just focusing on the presence of God. We usually have Christian music playing as we enter the Lord's throne room. David pleads, *"Do not cast me from your presence or take your Holy Spirit from me."* **This type of prayer is what the prayer team needs to employ; it is listening prayer.**

Gordon T. Smith declares,

> [Prayer] needs to be listening prayer. For so many, **prayer is talking to God rather than communion with God** ... Discerning prayer requires that at times **we simply shut up and remain silent in the presence of God.**[14] (Emphasis added.)

Often believers are too busy telling God what should transpire rather than being inspired by the Holy Spirit. The intercessors will be praying for the discernment of the Holy Spirit. The plan is based upon listening to God. This process takes time and cannot be rushed. God will provide direction.

During this time we are led by the Spirit into a time of confession, repentance and acknowledgement. In the presence of God our sins become apparent to us, and we confess that we are sinners in need of God's forgiveness. Many people don't feel worthy to pray because of their sins. When we confess our sins first, then our worthiness does not become an issue. We pray as David did,

> *Wash away all my iniquity and cleanse me from my sin. For I know my transgressions; and my sin is always before me.* — Psalm 51:2-3

During this time we feel the cleansing blood of Christ as we turn away from our sins and turn our focus completely on God our Savior. One of the sins I have confessed—and continue to confess as a pastor—is my focus on numbers, nickels and noses. This is not of God and does not lead to spiritual growth.

Prayer calls for humility. Ignatius Loyola states that humility is "seeing oneself in truth."[15] Humility naturally leads us into an acknowledgement that only God is God—we are not. He is holy and we are not. It seems as if most of the time we live our lives striving for control of our circumstances and life situations. In essence, we want to be God and usurp His rule and authority. On Monday evenings we surrender all control to God and acknowledge Him as Lord and God.

> *Have mercy on me, O God, according to your unfailing love; according to your great compassion blot out my transgressions ... so that you are proved right when you speak and justified when you judge.* — Psalm 51:1, 4b

God is all merciful, all loving, and all knowing. God is always right, so why do we fight so hard not to listen to Him? When I preach in the Maricopa County jails to inmates in stripes and pink underwear, I ask them how their lives are going when they are "large and in charge." They realize their bad choices have led to their incarceration, and are ready to hand over control of their lives to Jesus. This is a dramatic illustration, but do we not face the same choice every day?

In Psalm 5:5 David writes, *"The arrogant cannot stand in your presence. You hate all who do wrong."* We need to humbly confess our daily arrogance and acknowledge Jesus as our Lord as well as Savior. We need to stop fighting Him for control of our lives. Let Jesus take full control. He is God!

We pray earnestly to be filled with the Holy Spirit, and ask for more and more of His presence and power. Soon we are overwhelmed with the peace, power and presence of God. At these times we do not know if we have ascended to heaven or heaven has descended upon us.

When we surrender control to Jesus in our prayers and experience the presence of the Holy Spirit, we are led by the Holy Spirit to give thanks and praise Him. Then we pray like David, "*Restore to me the joy of your salvation and grant me a willing spirit, to sustain me."* On Monday evenings after we acknowledge Jesus as Lord of our lives many of us will sing or verbally praise Him and give thanks. Some will pray in tongues as the Spirit leads. Although some pray in tongues, it is definitely not a requirement to give thanks and praise. Many times these praises are accompanied with tears of joy. At this point, the Holy Spirit takes over and pours out a flood of petitions and prayer requests into our hearts and minds. We come like empty vessels not knowing what to pray and then suddenly after being in God's presence, the Spirit floods us with words of prayer. I believe this is what Saint Paul describes in Romans 8:26-27:

> *In the same way, the Spirit helps us in our weakness. We do not know what we ought to pray for, but the Spirit himself intercedes for us with groans that words cannot express. And he who searches our hearts knows the mind of the Spirit, because the Spirit intercedes for the saints in accordance with God's will.*

The Spirit prays for us and through us. Praying in tongues is NOT a requirement, but NOT prohibited. This is an amazing experience. It is as if we are in the dark and the Holy Spirit turns on the lights so we know how to proceed in prayer. Paul describes this in Romans 12:2:

> *Do not conform any longer to the pattern of this world, but be transformed by the renewing of your mind. Then you will be able to test and approve what God's will is—his good, pleasing and perfect will.*

This holy communion with God the Holy Spirit changes every false misconception we may have pertaining to prayer—especially the charge of prayer being boring.

We find ourselves praying for and experiencing healings, miracles, visions, words, signs and wonders. We pray to be changed and to be used by God for His purpose and glory.

During this time, we experience an overwhelming sense of God's presence, power and peace. As we pray, the power of the Holy Spirit usually intensifies within us and among us. This empowers us to pray with discernment and power.

Within Gordon T. Smith's teachings there are three factors for spiritual discernment: consolation, Scripture and emotion/reason. Spiritual discernment is founded in Jesus' words: "*My sheep know my voice, and I know them. They follow me*" (John 10: 27). Spiritual discernment involves hearing the voice of Jesus the Good Shepherd rather than the voice of Satan, the world or the flesh. According to Smith, discernment is "*a discriminating choice between two or more competing options. It is an act of judgment.*"[16]

Spiritual discernment is a choice between two goods. To choose evil is not an option. Smith expounds,

> Discernment is a discriminating choice between two or more good options ... Good or evil is not the question; rather, the challenge is to know what is best.[17]

It is a matter of choosing the better of two options. Evil, vengeful or sinful petitions are not options. Where the Spirit is, there is peace, truth and righteousness.

First, during our Monday evening prayers when we are filled with the living presence of God, we pray from a framework of consolation as Gordon T. Smith suggests. As the Spirit floods our minds with whom and what to pray for, this is a time of consolation as opposed to a time of desolation. Consolation is "any feeling of peace, joy, contentment or serenity. It is a sense of well-being, of all-rightness."[18] It is very difficult, if not impossible, to pray rightly in the Spirit if we are in a spirit of desolation. Desolation is:

> ...any feeling of anger, depression, discouragement or inner turmoil. Sometimes it may be a feeling of malaise, not a specific feeling or reaction, just inner discomfort or dis-ease."[19]

If members of the prayer team experience desolation, they need to spend more time in silent prayer. Other prayer warriors also can lay hands on them and intercede for them with prayers, groaning and perhaps the gift of tongues. I have yet to witness a time when someone has remained in a state of desolation at our Monday prayer meetings. Both the *pray-ers* and *pray-ees* are changed in this process.

However, there are many important church decisions that are made during desolation as opposed to consolation, which is why many churches make decisions they soon regret.

Second, in this discernment process, "Holy Scripture is the starting point and measuring rod for individual [and group] insight."[20] If the prayer team wants to hear the voice of Jesus, then every member must be in God's Word, studying it and reading it daily.

Again, many bad decisions have been made in the Church by people who are not in God's Word. Remaining in God's Word is the only way to arrive at the truth regarding the correct direction of our prayers and also eliminate evil as an option. Smith contends,

> The Spirit will never contradict Scripture. When we are faced with competing options, both or all of which may be good and valid options, what we will long for is communion with Christ by His Spirit.

> So if we have neglected the study of Scripture, we will be at a distinct disadvantage."[21]

God keeps His Word. The prayer team needs to keep His Word living, guiding and working in them.

Third, this discernment process involves emotions as well as reason. Smith explains,

> God does not have a mouth; He does not speak audibly. Rather, God speaks to us through our feelings, impressions left on our minds. But we must not equate the voice in our head with the voice of God. We rather discern God's word in the interpretation of these impressions. We discern by perceiving and evaluating the movements of the heart. In the end it will be reason that guides us—but reason comes to terms with the feelings and impressions that are left on our inner person."[22]

Prayer warriors use both reason and emotions. Emotions are not something to fear, but a means of listening to God. Emotions are to be embraced. The group will function with reason but also listen to their instinctual gut feelings, as this is one way that God speaks. I believe in recent years the church has lost its passion in prayer by stifling its emotions. All of the great church prayer warriors or mystics were passionate and emotional in their prayers. Today we have exalted our reason in prayer and removed the passion and fire from our prayers. Is it any wonder many Christians are reluctant to pray and find prayer boring?

Personally, I feel power in my hands. It usually leads me to lay on hands and pray for a particular person who is present, and that person feels the power of the Spirit enter through them. This is not from me but from God. There are also times when I have been the recipient of the power of the Holy Spirit when others have laid hands upon me and prayed for me.

At this point, some of you may be thinking like Martin Luther, "Rick, you've swallowed the Holy Spirit, feathers and all!" Well this is a possibility, but I know the Spirit is real and we can feel His presence and power.

Most recently, I visited Bruce, a middle-aged man, who had fallen from a 15-foot ladder, breaking both of his legs. Bruce was not a regular worship attendee, and did not consider himself a member of the church or even a Christian at this time. Paula, his wife and a disciple of Jesus, and I had been praying for Bruce for years. During my first visit I asked God to give Bruce visions or dreams of Jesus.

I visited him several times in the hospital, but after his second surgery Bruce shared the following experience with me. He described how on the previous day he felt so terrible that he wished he would just die. He was going to share this with his wife, Paula, but didn't because she had just come from a worship service and was very emotional after receiving some personal healing from God's presence.

Shortly after Paula arrived, Bruce vomited. He felt a little better at first, then suddenly felt a sensation of hundreds of small fingers physically touching him and healing the many places where he felt pain in his body. At the same time he felt he was being filled with power and a tremendous peace came upon him.

This is the peace of which Paul writes in Philippians 4:7: *"And the peace of God, which transcends all understanding, will guard your hearts and your minds in Christ Jesus."* The pain was gone. Bruce felt this power or energy surging through him, and even through the hospital bed. He was so filled with this power that he asked Paula and the nurse, who was a Christian, to hold his hands. He wanted them to feel this power and peace. Although they didn't feel the power, Bruce said Jesus had touched him and spoken to him. Jesus had told Bruce to tell everyone what He had done for him. Later when asked what Jesus voice sounded like, Bruce responded by saying Jesus simply sounded like a voice in a crowd.

After hearing Bruce's story I held his hand and prayed for him. Although I prayed for Bruce, I was the one who felt a download of God's power and peace. I was in a holy shock, and could hardly stand on my feet.

Since that visit, Pastor Perry has visited Bruce and experienced the same holy shock sensation. In follow-up visits, Bruce's pain was gone and he was at complete peace. The peace he experienced was physically visible.

Prayer had transformed Bruce. He told his story to everyone who entered his room. I continued to receive holy shocks when I prayed with him. Ironically, this happened at a time when I was discouraged and had asked God for some sign or green light. God answered my desperate plea in a big way, beyond my expectations, through Bruce.

The point is that God's power and presence are real. We can feel them and experience them, just as we experience the warmth of sunshine on an overcast day. Though the clouds may cover the sunshine for a time, eventually the sun will break through the clouds. This is how it is with us and the presence of God. The presence of God changed the person prayed for (Bruce) ***and*** those interceding (Paula, Pastor Perry, and me).

Plan on being changed when you pray! Prayer involves our emotions, senses and reason. Both pray-ers and pray-ees are favorably impacted by our prayers on Monday evenings.

Hazel, another senior member at Amazing Grace, has suffered from chronic back pain for 15 years. In fact, she could not even stand up straight. She shared this with Sandi, one of our prayer warriors. Sandi placed her hand on Hazel's back and prayed for healing. Hazel was skeptical, to say the least. However, the next day Hazel's back pain was gone, and has yet to return. Hazel was so excited that on Sunday she stood up during my sermon and testified to the healing power of Jesus through Sandi. This is way outside the box for Hazel, who is a lifetime Midwestern Lutheran. For Hazel, David's prayer was answered: *"Let me hear joy and gladness; let the bones you have crushed rejoice."*

Not long after Hazel's healing, we were assembled and praying on a Monday evening. During our vocal prayer time—after about an hour of listening prayer—I was offering up petitions when suddenly I felt hands on my back and heard the murmuring of someone praying for me. It was Sandi—she had felt led to pray for her pastors.

She prayed for me for quite some time and then went and laid on hands and prayed for Pastor Perry. However, when Sandi prayed for me, I felt power shoot through my spine. I was seated at the time, and the feeling was so intense that I felt I couldn't stand up even if I had wanted to. The power wasn't painful, but energizing, peaceful and soothing. After our prayer meeting Sandi affirmed that she had felt power flowing into me and Pastor Perry.

I recently had been diagnosed with arthritis in my spine and had suffered with chronic back pain for years. I had not requested prayer for my back, and Sandi was not praying specifically for my back pain. Later that week I noticed my back pain was gone, even though I had been moving furniture in our home. The pain has not returned. Our Lord Jesus had healed my back through Sandi's heartfelt prayer for her pastor.

After our time of intercession on Mondays, we may celebrate the Lord's Supper. We always sing a hymn and receive a benediction. We all leave with a tremendous feeling of peace and well-being, no matter how disheveled we were emotionally or spiritually upon our arrival. We experience what David prayed for in Psalm 51: "*the joy of your salvation and grant me a willing spirit, to sustain me.*" With the joy of our salvation and a willing spirit we are ready for mission.

I realize this may be a little too exuberant or wild for some, and perhaps too tame for others. But, this is our experience of prayer at our Monday evening prayer meetings. It is real and power-packed. Prayers and prayer times can take many forms. Choose the form that works best for you. Adapt what works, and improvise or improve where needed.

My last words on how to pray include two recommendations:

- Focus on the presence of God, and
- Do not fear your emotions.

These two points have transformed my personal prayer life and the prayer life of Amazing Grace. ***Taste and see that the Lord is good!***

DISCUSSION OR REFLECTION QUESTIONS

1. Who talks more during your prayer time, you or God? Do you spend time in listening prayer? Describe.

2. Discuss Psalm 46:10.

3. Have you ever been guided by the Spirit in prayer? Describe.

4. Do you pray in desolation or consolation? What are the results?

5. Do you use your emotions during prayer or stifle your emotions? Why or why not?

6. Have you experienced healings, miracles, visions, words, signs, and wonders? Please share with the group.

7. Share a time when you have felt the presence of God.

8. Can you start a prayer meeting in your church? Why not?

Chapter Five

Obedience and Prayer

Prayer requires obedience to God and to His Word. Obedience is not a very popular concept in today's culture. In the United States, we believe in individual rights and freedom, which in themselves are very good things. However, when we apply our individual rights above the will of Almighty God, then we have a serious problem in our lives and in our prayer lives.

Obedience to God in our prayer lives requires that we seek His face or call upon His name. Lack of obedience to God's command to seek Him is the reason many Christians and churches do not experience the power of God in their ministries and their lives.

J. Vernon McGee states, "A prayerless Christian is a powerless Christian."[23]

In 2 Chronicles 7:11-22, God makes it clear to Solomon that He requires obedience from His people:

> *When Solomon had finished the temple of the LORD and the royal palace, and had succeeded in carrying out all he had in mind to do in the temple of the LORD and in his own palace,*

the LORD appeared to him at night and said: "I have heard your prayer and have chosen this place for myself as a temple for sacrifices.

When I shut up the heavens so that there is no rain, or command locusts to devour the land or send a plague among my people,

if my people, who are called by my name, will humble themselves and pray and seek my face and turn from their wicked ways, then will I hear from heaven and will forgive their sin and will heal their land.

Now my eyes will be open and my ears attentive to the prayers offered in this place.

I have chosen and consecrated this temple so that my Name may be there forever. My eyes and my heart will always be there.

As for you, if you walk before me as David your father did, and do all I command, and observe my decrees and laws,

I will establish your royal throne, as I covenanted with David your father when I said, 'You shall never fail to have a man to rule over Israel.'

But if you turn away and forsake the decrees and commands I have given you and go off to serve other gods and worship them,

then I will uproot Israel from my land, which I have given them, and will reject this temple I have consecrated for my Name. I will make it a byword and an object of ridicule among all peoples.

And though this temple is now so imposing, all who pass by will be appalled and say, 'Why has the LORD done such a thing to this land and to this temple?'

People will answer, 'Because they have forsaken the LORD, the God of their fathers, who brought them out of Egypt, and have embraced other gods, worshiping and serving them—that is why he brought all this disaster on them.'"

Obedience to God brings blessing (not necessarily financial gain), while disobedience brings rejection. Rejection takes the form of the removal of God's loving presence from among His people. If we take time to think about God removing His presence from our lives, this in itself should be enough to bring us to our knees in prayer. However, disobedience in prayer does exist and takes form primarily in not seeking God's presence and being disobedient to His Word, or in other words, sinning.

We do not seek God's face. How much time do we devote to seeking God's face or calling upon His name in prayer every day? Add up the minutes—I believe the average Christian does not seek God's presence even five minutes per day. Is this obedience to God?

Samuel Chadwick writes,

> The one concern of the devil is to keep Christians from praying. He fears nothing from prayerless studies, prayerless work and prayerless religion. He laughs at our toil, mocks at our wisdom, but he trembles when we pray.[24]

The Scriptures are very clear:

> *In that day you will no longer ask me anything. I tell you the truth, my Father will give you whatever you ask in my name. 24Until now you have not asked for anything in my name.* **Ask and you will receive, and your joy will be complete.**
> — John 16:23-27 (Emphasis added.)

He will call upon me, and I will answer him; I will be with him in trouble, I will deliver him and honor him. — Psalm 91:15

You are forgiving and good, O Lord, abounding in love to all who call to you. — Psalm 86:5

The LORD is near to all who call on him, to all who call on him in truth. — Psalm 145:18

Those who know your name will trust in you, for you, LORD, have never forsaken those who seek you. — Psalm 9:10

You hear, O LORD, the desire of the afflicted; you encourage them, and you listen to their cry.
— Psalm 10:17

The eyes of the LORD are on the righteous and his ears are attentive to their cry;
the face of the LORD is against those who do evil, to cut off the memory of them from the earth.
The righteous cry out, and the LORD hears them; he delivers them from all their troubles.
— Psalm 34:15-17

In disobedience to God and His Word, we don't seek or call upon the Lord. We depend upon ourselves. After all, it is our right—or is it? Seek the Lord! Pray!

Alan Perkins writes:

> A man arrives in heaven, and St. Peter is showing him around. After a while, they pass by a large warehouse, and the man inquires what is inside. "Oh, you don't want to see that," protests St. Peter. The man's curiosity is piqued, and he demands to see inside. St. Peter opens the door, and they see a warehouse full of wonderful things, stacked

to the rafters. "Why didn't you want me to see this?" the man demands. "It all looks wonderful!" "Well," says St. Peter, "I thought it might make you sad. You see, those are all the things God had ready to give you, if you had only asked for them in prayer."[25]

What are we missing out on because we do not seek the presence of the Lord in prayer? No prayer, no power! Know prayer, know power!

Obedience in prayer involves obedience to God's law or Word. The Lord does not listen to the prayers of those deliberately living in sin. The Scriptures are clear:

> ***But if you turn away and forsake the decrees and commands I have given you and go off to serve other gods and worship them,***
>
> ***then I will uproot Israel from my land, which I have given them, and will reject this temple I have consecrated for my Name.*** *I will make it a byword and an object of ridicule among all peoples. (Emphasis added.)*
>
> — 2 Chronicles 7: 19-20

Our unconfessed sins and our lack of repentance is a blockage to our prayers. The Lord does not answer unrepentant sinners. None of us is without sin. But continual, deliberate, unrepentant disobedience to God's commands (or sin) will result in unanswered prayer. Even unbelievers are aware of this point. There are many times when unbelievers request prayer from Christians because they know God listens to those who honor Him and His Word.

> *We know that God does not listen to sinners. He listens to the godly man who does his will.*
>
> — John 9:31

Their deeds do not permit them to return to their God._ A spirit of prostitution is in their heart they do not acknowledge the LORD.

Israel's arrogance testifies against them; the Israelites, even Ephraim, stumble in their sin; Judah also stumbles with them.

When they go with their flocks and herd to seek the LORD, they will not find him he has withdrawn himself from them. — Hosea 5:4-6

They made their hearts as hard as flint and would not listen to the law or to the words that the LORD Almighty had sent by his Spirit through the earlier prophets. So the LORD Almighty was very angry.

"When I called, they did not listen; so when they called, I would not listen," says the LORD Almighty.
— Zechariah 7:12-13

But your iniquities have separated you from your God; your sins have hidden his face from you, so that he will not hear. — Isaiah 59:2

The LORD is far from the wicked but he hears the prayer of the righteous. — Proverbs 15:29

Therefore confess your sins to each other and pray for each other so that you may be healed. The prayer of a righteous man is powerful and effective. — James 5:16

...and receive from him anything we ask, because we obey his commands and do what pleases him.
— 1 John 3:22

Husbands, in the same way be considerate as you live with your wives, and treat them with respect as the weaker partner and as heirs with you of the gracious gift of life, so that nothing will hinder your prayers. — 1 Peter 3:7

From these Scriptures we can conclude that sin affects our family relationships, and overall sin is an obstacle to prayer. This is why the Spirit always leads us into confession and forgiveness before we enter the throne of God.

An example of power in a repentant person's prayers comes from an inmate. I serve as a religious volunteer in the Maricopa County Jail in Arizona. I find preaching in the jails gratifying and very uplifting. The inmates come to worship because they want to be there. Sometimes they have to endure handcuffs, leg shackles, or being strip-searched (by officers of the opposite sex) in order to hear God's Word. But they come and listen, knowing they are sinners in need of Jesus Christ. They are very fertile soil for the Gospel. Does God answer their prayers? Absolutely!

One inmate was standing before a judge with a prison officer ready to take him away to serve five years in prison. The judge shared that previously she had decided to send him away to state prison. But at the last minute, she said she could always send him to prison next time. He received two years probation.

I always ask the inmates to pray for Amazing Grace and for me. There is power in a repentant person's prayers. If only the people in the church pews prayed with such fervor and repentance; we could prevail against the very gates of hell! We need to acknowledge our sinfulness before we pray and to ask to be washed in the blood of Jesus.

Our failure to forgive others is also a blockage to our prayers. What has God commanded regarding forgiveness? The Scriptures are very clear:

So they sent word to Joseph, saying, "Your father left these instructions before he died:

'This is what you are to say to Joseph: ***I ask you to forgive your brothers the sins and the wrongs they committed in treating you so badly.*** *'* ***Now please forgive the sins of the servants of the God of your father***." *When their message came to him, Joseph wept.*

— Genesis 50:16-17

But I tell you that anyone who is angry with his brother will be subject to judgment. Again, anyone who says to his brother, "Raca," is answerable to the Sanhedrin. But anyone who says, "You fool!" will be in danger of the fire of hell.

Therefore, if you are offering your gift at the altar and there remember that your brother has something against you,

leave your gift there in front of the altar. First go and be reconciled to your brother; then come and offer your gift. — Matthew 5:22-24

In anger his master turned him over to the jailers to be tortured, until he should pay back all he owed.

"This is how my heavenly Father will treat each of you unless you forgive your brother from your heart." — Matthew 18:34-35

Therefore I tell you, whatever you ask for in prayer, believe that you have received it, and it will be yours.

And when you stand praying, if you hold anything against anyone, forgive him, so that your Father in heaven may forgive you your sins."

— Mark 11:24-25

Our prayers fail because we fail to forgive! It is difficult for the Holy Spirit to enter into a heart that is hardened by unforgiveness. George Herbert said, *"He who cannot forgive others breaks the bridge over which he must pass."*[26]

Keith, a brother in Christ, was counseling a woman in a wheelchair. She couldn't walk because the doctors had to fuse her pelvis to her hips due to an accident. She asked Keith why God had not answered her prayers. A word of knowledge came to Keith by the Holy Spirit and he said she needed to forgive her father. Keith did not know what needed to be forgiven, he simply spoke the word. Keith prayed with the woman and left.

Later the woman called Keith on the telephone in tears. She was standing by her kitchen sink and she could now walk. She cried, and said that she had forgiven her father and now she could walk. As she was talking to Keith on the phone, her husband came in the kitchen and was amazed that his wife was standing. He hugged his wife and they tearfully danced in the kitchen while Keith was still on the line.

An unforgiving heart is a blockage to our prayers. As you are reading this, perhaps someone has come to mind that you have not forgiven or against whom you hold a grudge. Please make time ***now*** to fall on your knees and ask the Holy Spirit to help you forgive this person. If you don't know what to say, here is a sample prayer to pray:

> Lord God, I seek your face. I enter your presence and I ask you to forgive me my sins. I also ask that You forgive this person or persons who have hurt me. I ask that You empower me to forgive them from my heart. I ask that you bless them ... let them know the joy of your salvation. In Jesus name, Amen!

If possible, remain on your knees until you feel the burden of hate depart from you. If not, the next time you pray, invite the Holy Spirit again into your heart to change you. Eventually, the Lord will remove this burden.

Another key blockage to prayer is pride. We feel we are self-sufficient and don't need God. We may believe only weak or crazy people pray for God's help. I thank God I am crazy for Jesus!

Contrary to this type of thinking, the Scriptures are clear:

> *If my people, who are called by my name,* ***will humble themselves*** *and pray and seek my face and turn from their wicked ways, then will I hear from heaven and will forgive their sin and will heal their land.* (Emphasis added.)
>
> — 2 Chronicles 7:14

> *Love the Lord, all his saints! The Lord preserves the faithful,* **but the proud he pays back in full.** (Emphasis added.) — Psalm 31:23

> *Though the Lord is on high, he looks upon the lowly,* **but the proud he knows from afar.** (Emphasis added.) — Psalm 138:6

> But he gives us more grace. That is *why Scripture says: "God opposes the proud but gives grace to the humble."* — James 4:6

> *He does not answer when men cry out because of the arrogance of the wicked.* — Job 35:12

> *Going a little farther, he fell with his face to the ground and prayed, "My Father, if it is possible, may this cup be taken from me. Yet not as I will, but as you will."* — Matthew 26:39

At this, Job got up and tore his robe and shaved his head. Then he fell to the ground in worship and said: "Naked I came from my mother's womb, and naked I will depart. — Job 1:20-21

The LORD hears the needy and does not despise his captive people. — Psalm 69:33

Our pride or lack of humility keeps us from seeking the Lord. We must ***humble ourselves before the Lord!*** Brothers and sisters, where has the humility gone in the church? Not just in prayer, but in every aspect of church life? I believe pastors are the worst offenders—especially in regard to Scripture! We pompously believe we have the correct meaning as ***we*** interpret God's Word. The truth is, ***God's Word*** should be interpreting and transforming us. God's Word boldly declares in 1 Corinthians 1:19-20:

For it is written: "I will destroy the wisdom of the wise; the intelligence of the intelligent I will frustrate."

Where is the wise man? Where is the scholar? Where is the philosopher of this age? Has not God made foolish the wisdom of the world?

Martin Luther was emphatic on remaining humble in prayer and approaching the Scriptures. Here is one of my favorite Luther quotes regarding pride:

If, however, you feel and are inclined to think you have made it, flattering yourself with your own little books, teaching, or writing, because you have done it beautifully and preached excellently; if you are highly pleased when someone praises you in the presence of others; if you perhaps look for praise, and would sulk or quit what you are doing if you did not get it—if you are of that

> stripe, dear friend, then take yourself by the ears, and if you do this the right way you will find a beautiful pair of big, long, shaggy donkey ears. Then do not spare any expense! Decorate them with golden bells, so that people will be able to hear you wherever you go, point their fingers at you, and say, **"See, see! There goes that clever beast, who can write such exquisite books and preach so remarkably well" ... Let us be proud and seek honor in the places we can. But in this book the honor is God's alone, as it is said, "God opposes the proud, but gives grace to the humble"** (1Peter 5:5); **to whom be glory, world without end, Amen."**[27]
> (Emphasis added.)

There is no place for pride in prayer or in the Christian life. We need to realize we are completely dependent upon God for ***all*** things, including the words we pray.

Perhaps the greatest obstacle to prayer is our lack of trust and hope in God. *"Now my eyes will be open and my ears attentive to the prayers offered in this place"* (2 Chronicles 7:15). This is God's promise to us. And He makes this promise to us repeatedly in His Word. We simply do not believe God's promises. We do not **trust** Him!

> *Let us **draw near to God with a sincere heart in full assurance of faith**, having our hearts sprinkled to cleanse us from a guilty conscience and having our bodies washed with pure water.*
> — Hebrews 10:22 (Emphasis added.)

> ***This is the confidence we have in approaching God:*** *that if we ask anything according to his will, he hears us.*

And if ***we know that he hears us—whatever we ask—we know that we have what we asked of him.*** — 1 John 5:14-15 (Emphasis added.)

If any of you lacks wisdom, he should ask God, who gives generously to all without finding fault, and it will be given to him.

But when he asks, ***he must believe and not doubt, because he who doubts is like a wave of the sea, blown and tossed by the wind.***

That man should not think he will receive anything from the Lord*...* — James 1:5-7 (Emphasis added.)

And I will do whatever you ask in my name, so that the Son may bring glory to the Father.

You may ask me for anything in my name, and I will do it. — John 14:13-14 (Emphasis added.)

If you believe, you will receive whatever you ask for in prayer." — Matthew 21:22 (Emphasis added.)

"For I know the plans I have for you," declares the *Lord*, **"plans to prosper you and not to harm you, plans to give you hope and a future.**

Then you will call upon me and come and pray to me, and I will listen to you."

— Jeremiah 29:11-12 (Emphasis added.)

Delight yourself in the Lord and he will give you the desires of your heart.

Commit your way to the Lord; trust in him and he will do this: — Psalm 37:4-5

I wait for you, O Lord; you will answer, O Lord my God. — Psalm 38:15

The Lord looked down from his sanctuary on high, from heaven he viewed the earth,

to hear the groans of the prisoners and release those condemned to death." — Psalm 102:19-20

God wants us to pray believing in His love and power to accomplish what He promises. There are many situations and circumstances that seem impossible for us. In fact, they actually may ***be*** impossible for us. But **nothing** is impossible for our God. We have a very **big God**. Trust in Him in all things and pray big prayers.

Pastor Daniel Banja, who is an apostle in Uganda, came to Amazing Grace and shared the following story in a sermon. Pastor Daniel ministers in the rural areas of Uganda and not in the cities. He is the shepherd of 32 churches, and goes to the far-off villages and tribes to preach the Gospel. His audience is usually animistic, but at times Muslim.

One day he was preaching in a rural village that was pagan and animistic, and the band was playing music behind him. Suddenly, the tribal chieftain came before him with a crowd carrying stones. They were dragging a woman with them who was completely blind in one eye. The chieftain demanded that Pastor Daniel heal her immediately or they would stone him to death.

Pastor Daniel looked behind himself for the church music group. They all had run away. Pastor Daniel prayed to heaven and placed his hand on the woman's eye and commanded with these words, "*Woman! In the name of Jesus, SEE!*" At that instant, the woman could see! She started dancing and thanking Daniel and praising his God. The chieftain and the entire village became Christian and were baptized, and another church was started. I don't know if the music group ever came back. Brothers and sisters, pray believing!

DISCUSSION OR REFLECTION QUESTIONS

1. How obedient to God's command regarding prayer are you? How can you improve your prayer life?

2. J. Vernon McGee states, "A prayerless Christian is a powerless Christian." Would you describe yourself as prayerful and powerful or as prayerless and powerless?

3. Do you regularly seek the Lord or do you depend on your own counsel? Why or why not?

4. Read Judges 7. Do you trust God's promises and power like Gideon? Why or why not?

5. What are the main obstacles that keep you from prayer?

Chapter Six

Awareness of God and His Timing

In the last few years as we have prayed on Monday evenings, we have all developed a keener awareness of God's presence in our lives and a greater understanding of God's timing. We all know God is omnipresent, which quite simply means He is infinite and present everywhere at the same time.

But what is most important is being aware of God's presence in our own lives. God is with us 24 hours a day, seven days a week—but how often are we aware of His presence or in conversation with Him? In a 24-hour period, how much time do we live knowingly in awareness of Jesus' presence with us and in us?

Living in God's presence is a theme throughout the Scriptures. As we look at Scripture, generally, being in God's presence is a good thing—but not always.

> *The LORD replied, "**My Presence will go with you, and I will give you rest**."*
>
> — Exodus 33:14 (Emphasis added)

And the LORD said, ***"I will cause all my goodness to pass in front of you, and I will proclaim my name, the LORD, in your presence. I will have mercy on whom I will have mercy, and I will have compassion on whom I will have compassion."*** — Exodus 33:19 (Emphasis added.)

But whenever he entered the LORD's presence to speak with him, he removed the veil until he came out. *And when he came out and told the Israelites what he had been commanded.*
— Exodus 34:34 (Emphasis added.)

Instead, you are to ***eat them in the presence of the LORD your God at the place the LORD your God will choose—you, your sons and daughters, your menservants and maidservants, and the Levites from your towns—and you are to rejoice before the LORD your God in everything you put your hand to.*** — Deuteronomy 12:18
(Emphasis added.)

Yet give attention to your servant's prayer and his plea for mercy, O LORD my God. ***Hear the cry and the prayer that your servant is praying in your presence.*** — 2 Chronicles 6:19
(Emphasis added.)

The king stood by his pillar and renewed the covenant in the presence of the LORD— *to follow the LORD and keep his commands, regulations and decrees with all his heart and all his soul, and to obey the words of the covenant written in this book.* — 2 Chronicles 34:31
(Emphasis added.)

You have made known to me the path of life; ***you will fill me with joy in your presence,*** *with eternal pleasures at your right hand.* (Emphasis added.) — Psalm 16:11

In the shelter of your presence you hide them from the intrigues of men; *in your dwelling you keep them safe from accusing tongues.* (Emphasis added.) — Psalm 31:20

Arise, cry out in the night, as the watches of the night begin; pour out your heart like water in the presence of the Lord. Lift up your hands to him for the lives of your children, who faint from hunger at the head of every street. — Lamentations 2:19

You have made known to me the paths of life; you will fill me with joy in your presence.
— Acts 2:28

This then is how we know that we belong to the truth, *and how we set our hearts at rest in his presence*

whenever our hearts condemn us. For God is greater than our hearts, and he knows everything.
— 1 John 3:19-20

It is evident in the Scriptures that we should want to live continually in God's presence. It is interesting that this is not an emphasis in many congregations today, and at times sharing about the presence of God is frowned upon or even considered crazy. Was Moses crazy? Was King David a whacko? Was Paul deranged? The answer to these questions is yes! They had a divine insanity that is greater than the greatest wisdom of the world. They experienced the presence of the living God. They lived in the kingdom of God.

Our model as Christians is Jesus, who lived His entire life in awareness of God's presence. Is there any wonder why Jesus could heal the sick, calm the storm, confound the teachers of the law and raise the dead? He lived His life in communion with God. Imagine how wonderful that would be! Jesus declares in John 7:28-29:

> *Yes, you know me, and you know where I am from. I am not here on my own, but he who sent me is true. You do not know him,*
>
> *but I know him because I am from him and he sent me."*

Jesus was continually aware of the Father's presence in His life.

Now, through Jesus, we can experience that same presence of the living God in our lives. Jesus makes this clear to us in John 17: 24-26:

> *Father, I want those you have given me to be with me where I am, and to see my glory, the glory you have given me because you loved me before the creation of the world.*
>
> *Righteous Father, though the world does not know you,* ***I know you, and they know that you have sent me.***
>
> ***I have made you known to them, and will continue to make you known in order that the love you have for me may be in them and that I myself may be in them.***

Do we realize what we have in Jesus? We have God's abiding presence. This has been Pastor Perry and my greatest learning experience the past few years at our Monday evening prayer meetings. We experience God in such a powerful way on Mondays that it carries through the entire week. We love God's presence in our lives!

It has also enriched our worship at Amazing Grace. There are times we cannot even stand up because of the overwhelming presence of God. There is no time limit on prayer or worship, and no one watches the clock. We are in a holy time warp. A worship service that goes an hour and 40 minutes seems to be 15 minutes long. Two hours of prayer in the presence of God seems like ten minutes.

Pastor Perry and I are working on taking our minds off numbers and focusing on Jesus' presence. Have we lost some mmbers? Yes. Have we gained some members? Yes. Are we making our budget? Yes, by God's marvelous grace. Most importantly, are we making disciples? Yes.

Friends, we are living the ever-changing adventure of Jesus! Is it always smooth sailing? No. I tell people I have two lines of people in my life. One line consists of those people who hate me, and the other line consists of those who love me. Both lines are getting longer. I just hope the line of lovers is longer.

I have been called to be a pastor, an equipper of the saints. I have not been called to be a people pleaser. The greater church needs to learn this. Pastors are to be loved and respected. But there are times when your pastor should challenge you—and perhaps even get you a little hot under the collar. However, if pastor and congregation are both realizing the kingdom of God, then the other stuff is just stuff. It is non-essential because living in Jesus' presence offsets everything else. Friends, there is nothing on heaven or earth like dwelling in the presence of Almighty God: Father, Son, and Holy Spirit!

Maybe you have not experienced the presence of God during your prayers and are feeling disappointed with your prayer life. My advice is just keep on praying!

Roseann is a member of our church who works as a bus driver. She prayed during the day on her bus, but felt that God was far away and was not listening to her. She was ready to give up with prayer. Then one day as she was praying on her bus, she felt God's presence. She felt warmth come over her body and felt completely at peace. She knew Jesus loved her and He was with her. Now she prays all day long on her bus. She prays for her passengers, other drivers, passersby and even for stray cats. She has realized God's presence in prayer and talks with Him all day. If your prayer life is dry, just keep on praying. God will answer you in a variety of marvelous ways.

As we live and pray in God's presence, we get a clearer picture of God's timing. Jesus states in John 7:6-8:

> *Therefore Jesus told them,* ***"The right time for me has not yet come; for you any time is right.***
>
> *The world cannot hate you, but it hates me because I testify that what it does is evil.*
>
> *You go to the Feast.* ***I am not yet going up to this Feast, because for me the right time has not yet come."***

Because of Jesus' communion with the Father and Holy Spirit, He had a firm grasp on God's timeline. He knew who He was, where He was going and when He should go. Usually, we know God's timing after the fact. But Jesus knew God's timing exactly.

> *Jesus answered, "Even if I testify on my own behalf,* ***my testimony is valid, for I know where I came from and where I am going****. But you have no idea where I come from or where I am going.* — John 8:14 (Emphasis added.)

> *Jesus,* ***knowing all that was going to happen to him****, went out and asked them, "Who is it you want?"* — John 18:4 (Emphasis added.)

Imagine if we could know God's perfect timing. Wow! Can we understand God's time exactly and immediately like Jesus did? No. However, we can learn to see more of God's timing after the fact—and most importantly in our daily lives. Here are some wonderful examples of God's timing as found in the Scriptures:

> *Joseph said to his brothers, "I am Joseph! Is my father still living?" But his brothers were not able to answer him, because they were terrified at his presence.*
>
> *Then Joseph said to his brothers, "Come close to me." When they had done so, he said, "I am your brother Joseph, the one you sold into Egypt!*
>
> ***And now, do not be distressed and do not be angry with yourselves for selling me here, because it was to save lives that God sent me ahead of you.***
>
> *For two years now there has been famine in the land, and for the next five years there will be no plowing and reaping. [7] But God sent me ahead of you to preserve for you a remnant on earth and to save your lives by a great deliverance*.
>
> ***So then, it was not you who sent me here, but God. He made me father to Pharaoh, lord of his entire household and ruler of all Egypt.***
>
> *Now hurry back to my father and say to him, 'This is what your son Joseph says: God has made me lord of all Egypt. Come down to me; don't delay.*
>
> *You shall live in the region of Goshen and be near me—you, your children and grandchildren, your flocks and herds, and all you have.*
>
> — Genesis 45:3-10 (Emphasis added.)

This is what the L*ORD says: "**In the time of my favor I will answer you, and in the day of salvation I will help you**; I will keep you and will make you to be a covenant for the people, to restore the land and to reassign its desolate inheritances..."* — Isaiah 49:8
(Emphasis added.)

*You see, **at just the right time**, when we were still powerless, Christ died for the ungodly.* (Emphasis added.) — Romans 5:6

It is very difficult, if not impossible, to discern God's timing while going through certain situations. Like Joseph being sold into slavery by his brothers, there are many times we must wait and see what God is doing. God is faithful and He will reveal His will to us in His time. And for His time, we may have to wait until we are with Him in heaven. Have you ever been frustrated by God's timing? Have you ever prayed as David prayed?

How long, L*ORD? Will you forget me forever? How long will you hide your face from me?*

— Psalm 13:1

Since this is my favorite Psalm, you can see my own struggles with God's timing. Do you struggle with God's timing? This past year, I visited Jim, a former truck driver, when he was in the hospital. He was in his late 60s, but was on oxygen due to congestive heart failure and emphysema. Jim came to worship with a small oxygen tank and wore the breathing tubes that wrapped over his ears and under his nose. Jim had entered the hospital during December, and I would visit him and bring him Holy Communion.

I visited Jim the week after Christmas. As usual, he was in bed with an oxygen mask on, and happened to be watching the television. When he saw me, Jim turned off the television and started weeping. I usually don't have this effect on people. He called me to his bedside and said he'd had the best Christmas ever. Still crying, Jim said that as parents there are times we make mistakes. He told me that 13 years ago he had fought to get custody of his granddaughter from his daughter.

His daughter and son-in-law were doing hard drugs and Jim did not want his granddaughter exposed to such a dangerous environment. His daughter and son-in-law fled the state for California. They quit doing drugs, bought a home and resumed a normal family life.

But for 13 years his daughter would have nothing to do with Jim—until Christmas day, when his daughter called him in his hospital room. She talked and they made amends, and then he was able to speak with his now 15-year-old granddaughter. He'd had no contact with this granddaughter for 13 years. They promised to make arrangements to come and visit Jim in Arizona. Jim continued to weep and said it was the best Christmas in his entire life.

Jim went on to say that Amazing Grace had made all the difference. The prayers of the church and the presence of God had changed his life. He would never be the same. And he wasn't. Jim asked me to tell everyone. The reconciliation between Jim and his daughter came while Jim was on his deathbed and in God's perfect timing.

I believe we learn patience through prayer in the throne room of God. We learn our concept of time and God's timing is completely different.

> *But do not forget this one thing, dear friends:*
> ***With the Lord a day is like a thousand years, and a thousand years are like a day.***
>
> ***The Lord is not slow in keeping his promise, as some understand slowness. He is patient***

with you, not wanting anyone to perish, but everyone to come to repentance.
— 2 Peter 3:8-9 (Emphasis added.)

In God's presence we see and experience the Kingdom of God. According to Scripture, everything is very different in the Kingdom of God—and in some cases the opposite of what we see, know and experience in our physical world. God's kingdom is here—but do we have eyes to see it and ears to hear it?

Paul writes in 2 Corinthians 4:18,

So we fix our eyes not on what is seen, but on what is unseen. For what is seen is temporary, but what is unseen is eternal.

There is an entire world surrounding us—the kingdom of God—filled with angels and demons and divine manifestations. To see what is taking place in the kingdom of God requires divine wisdom and patience. However, the more we pray, the more we see God's reign and timing.

One of the benefits of serving in the jails is the opportunity to see God's perfect timing. Some time ago I met Hector, at our Spanish jail worship. He was only in jail for about three months, but he faithfully came to worship. Hector lived in Amazing Grace's neighborhood, so upon his release he started attending worship services and later joined the church.

At about the same time, we had our third laptop computer stolen when someone broke into our sanctuary. The thieves broke in through a tall, narrow window, one of six spaced about ten feet apart on each side of our sanctuary. For years, the windows were filled with colored plastic crinkle glass, a poor man's stained glass. This made it easy to break into our sanctuary and steal our laptop computers. The leadership voted to replace the colored glass with glass blocks to lighten the sanctuary and to prevent further break-ins. The problem was that we were short of cash and couldn't afford a contractor.

I discovered Hector was a handyman and asked him if he could do the job. He volunteered to install the glass block at no charge. The windows turned out perfectly, even though Hector had never worked with glass block before. The new windows have transformed our sanctuary into a place of light. Since installing the windows, Hector's wife and children have started worshipping with him, and his youngest daughter, Aleena, was baptized. It is clear to see God's timing in this situation—here are some of the God factors:

- *Hector was incarcerated where our jail church was located at the right time.*
- *For the first time in years, Hector attended a worship service where I preached in Spanish.*
- *Hector lived close to our church.*
- *After his release, Hector not only came to our church but joined us.*
- *We were robbed shortly after Hector's release.*
- *We had no money and Hector worked for free.*
- *The replacement windows turned out perfectly, even though Hector had never worked with glass block before.*
- *Hector's family joined our church.*
- *Aleena was baptized, although the family came from another church tradition.*

None of these things were planned by Hector, Amazing Grace or me. The secular world would just call this a series of coincidences. Brothers and sisters, we believe this was the hand of God working marvelously with God's perfect timing. This is just one example, but when we live in the kingdom of God, we see God working continually and frequently.

My hope is that when you enter the presence of King Jesus in prayer, you, too, will experience the kingdom of God and see the wonders our God is performing every day. I will close this chapter with the words of David:

> ***I waited patiently for the Lord; he turned to me and heard my cry.*** — Psalm 40:1
> (Emphasis added.)

DISCUSSION OR REFLECTION QUESTIONS:

1. How often are you aware of the presence of God in a 24-hour period? How can you improve your awareness?

2. Read Psalm 63:2-4. Describe a time when you have felt the overwhelming presence of God, What did you see, hear or feel?

3. Have you ever been frustrated by God's timing? Please share with the group.

4. Describe a time in your life when you have seen God's perfect timing.

5. Discuss a situation or event in our physical world that unbelievers attribute to coincidence, but believers know is the hand of God at work.

Conclusion

I hope you have enjoyed our journey in prayer and the astonishing presence of God. As stated at the beginning of the book, I am not a spiritual giant or guru. I am a simple urban pastor on a journey with Jesus. During our time together, we have learned what prayer is and what it is not. Prayer is not just a reverent petition to a deity. Prayer is so much more.

Prayer is seeking the Lord, entering His presence through Jesus Christ, and having a heart-to-heart conversation with God guided by the Holy Spirit that leads to transformation.

Prayer is the greatest blessing and privilege Almighty God has granted us. Through Jesus Christ, we can enter into the King's throne room and abide in His presence. This is the most miraculous thing—that we lowly human beings can dwell in the presence of our Holy God.

Furthermore, through the Holy Spirit, God speaks to us, guides us and actually gives us the words to pray. Through this encounter, we are continually being transformed into the image of Christ. We are not talking about some bland, tame experience. What we are talking about is an incredible spiritual journey in which we experience the love, peace and power of our infinite Creator.

Please join in this ever-changing adventure. Make time to pray. Start a prayer service at your church. Don't be dismayed if you are the only one there—the Lord will raise up an Aaron or Hur for you. We have His Word on it. Read His promise:

> *If my people, who are called by my name,* ***will humble themselves and pray and seek my face and turn from their wicked ways, then will I hear from heaven and will forgive their sin and will heal their land.***
>
> ***Now my eyes will be open and my ears attentive to the prayers offered in this place.***
>
> ***I have chosen and consecrated this temple so that my Name may be there forever. My eyes and my heart will always be there.***
> — 2 Chronicles 7:14-16 (Emphasis added.)

This is God speaking directly to us. Please believe Him and enter His presence. Enter into the spiritual battle. I truly believe that if every church dedicates itself to prayer, God will change the world. Pastor Perry says the darkness is getting darker in the world; but at the same time the light is getting brighter. I believe this is true.

Enter into the light of prayer and receive the fire of renewal in the Holy Spirit. Jesus is waiting for you. What are you waiting for?

DISCUSSION OR REFLECTION QUESTIONS

1. What has been your greatest learning from this journey?

2. How do you plan to change your prayer life?

3. How will you help your church to become a prayer station?

4. How has your group changed throughout this journey?

5. Read Mark 10:14-15. How have you experienced the kingdom of God on this journey?

End Notes

1 Jim Cymbala, *Fresh Wind, Fresh Fire* (Grand Rapids: Zondervan Publishing House, 1997), 182.

2 Gordon T. Smith, *Listening to God* (Downers Grove, IL: InterVarsity Press, 1997), 52.

3 E. Stanley Jones, in *Liberating Ministry From The Success Syndrome*, K. Hughes, Tyndale, 1988, 73.

4 Ibid, 41.

5 Ibid, 48.

6 Smith, *The Voice of Jesus*, 31.

7 Edwin Keith is a contributor on staff at: *Sermoncentral.com.*

8 As quoted in *Just Like Jesus*, Max Lucado, 71.

9 Illustration used by Mike Wilkins, a *Sermon Central* contributor.

10 Thomas G. Long, *Whispering The Lyrics*, CSS Publishing Company. http://www.eSermons.com.

11 Walter C. Hobbs, "Dependence on the Holy Spirit," in *Treasures in Clay Jars*, ed. by Lois Y. Barrett (Grand